Evermore

AN EMILY CHAMBERS SPIRIT MEDIUM NOVEL
#3

C.J. ARCHER

ISBN 978-0-9873372-5-2

FOR

For everyone who believes.

.

CHAPTER 1

London, Spring 1880

"Something's wrong," said the spirit of Lord Fulham.

"So I see." I squinted at the flickering entity standing beside the piano in Lady Willoughby's drawing room. The seven members of my audience watched me as I focused on the ghost they could neither see nor hear. Whether their expressions were mostly curious or afraid or a little of both, I didn't notice. I was much too intent on Lord Fulham.

He had been seventy-two when he'd died but was still a tall figure, albeit shaped like a wine barrel with a round, full middle. Yet he was not an imposing spirit. He trembled like a flame fighting a draught and was as transparent as a piece of fine muslin. I had never met a spirit that manifested so poorly.

"Are you about to cross?" I asked him.

He gave a nervous shake of his head. "I can't. None of us can."

"None?"

"I cannot stay here. It's much too difficult." His voice drifted off along with his body, but only for a moment before both returned even weaker. "The effort...costs...too much..." His wide eyes implored me, but to what end, I didn't know. If he weren't a ghost, I'd say he looked afraid, but what could a dead man possibly fear?

I was about to ask him when he disappeared altogether.

"Lord Fulham! Lord Fulham, return to me, please. Your loved ones wish to speak with you."

Nothing.

"Emily?" whispered my sister, Celia, sitting beside me at the table. "Is everything all right? You look like you've seen a... Oh, never mind."

Cold dread prickled my skin. Summoning spirits was an imprecise activity. Some had already crossed over to the Otherworld and could not hear my call, let alone act upon it. Others didn't want to revisit the living and simply ignored me. But never had I known ghosts that heard my call and wanted to come but could not.

Until yesterday. Lord Fulham was the second ghost in two days who had not been able to remain in our realm.

"Emily?" Celia prompted. "Is Lord Fulham's spirit with us?"

"He was," I said. "But he's gone."

"Gone where?" Lady Preston asked from her position on the opposite side of the table. The elegant countess clutched the hand of her friend, our hostess and Lord Fulham's daughter, Lady Willoughby, sitting next to her. The unease in her voice tugged at me. Lady Preston was particularly sensitive about communicating with the dead, having lost her son Jacob and then finding him again through me. Or, more accurately, she'd found his spirit.

"He has returned to the Waiting Area." I turned to my audience, which consisted of Celia plus six ladies from the upper echelons of London Society. It was the most elite séance we'd ever had, thanks to Lady Preston who'd suggested our services to Lady Willoughby. I didn't like disappointing them, but what else could I do?

"I'm sorry, Lady Willoughby." I gave her a sympathetic smile that I'd seen Celia use many times with the bereaved.

She was very good when it came to death and dealing with mourners. Quite an expert, in fact. Undertakers could learn much from her simple, heart-felt gestures. I was the only one aware that she was acting. "He would like to speak to you," I went on, "but he...needs to crossover."

I congratulated myself on a lie well told. Not a single one of the audience appeared to disbelieve me. They did, however, seem disappointed to be missing out on the spectacle of objects moving around the drawing room, and indeed Lady Willoughby sniffed into her handkerchief. She had dearly wanted to speak to her father.

Only Celia frowned in puzzlement. She was still frowning when Lady Willoughby rose and tugged the bell cord for tea.

"What a shame," said Adelaide Beaufort, Lady Preston's daughter, sitting on my other side at the small rectangular table. She and I were the same age and had developed a friendship in the previous weeks once it became known I'd communicated with her brother's ghost. "I believe Lady Willoughby wanted to ask her father where he'd hidden the key to his wine cellar. No one can find it, you see, and he had a very fine collection."

As she spoke, my gaze drifted to Lady Willoughby herself. Our hostess straightened, wrinkled her nose as if she smelled something off, and turned her shoulder to me.

"She doesn't look too disappointed anymore," I muttered. "Adelaide, did your mother find it difficult to convince Lady Willoughby to host this event?"

Adelaide studied her fingernails. An avoidance tactic if ever I saw one. "A little." She cringed. "Sorry, I shouldn't tell you."

"No, it's all right. I thought she seemed enthusiastic at first, but now...now she looks at me as if I were a fraud."

"Oh, Emily. You're not a fraud. Mother and I both know it. Forget what others think."

I smiled as sweetly as I could. "Of course." But I couldn't forget. Celia's and my independence depended upon the public believing us. Our income wasn't particularly high, but we had begun to make good money thanks to Lady Preston urging her friends to engage us. Sometimes we had two bookings during the day and another in the evening, quite unheard of until now. I liked to be busy. It kept me from thinking about Jacob Beaufort and that I hadn't seen him since we'd sent a rather horrible ghost back two weeks ago after he possessed a number of our friends.

I missed him. I felt hollow without him, like an empty shell washed up on the shore.

"Once they see you having a conversation with a ghost, they'll know that you are a genuine medium," Adelaide went on. She watched the other guests beneath half-lowered lashes, a stern set to her brow that defied anyone to question my authenticity. She was like a bulldog, albeit a pretty, blonde one.

"It's hard to have a conversation with a spirit when they cannot talk to you for very long," I said, pretending not to notice the way all the other guests avoided my gaze.

"Lord Fulham couldn't stay?" Adelaide asked.

"No. The same thing happened with another spirit yesterday. Neither she nor Lord Fulham had the strength to remain. There is something happening in the Waiting Area. Both appeared more faded than usual and neither was able to appear for long. Lord Fulham said it was too difficult." I didn't tell her about the frightened look on his face. It was a look that had unsettled me, but I saw no reason to worry Adelaide.

"Jacob will know more," Adelaide said with certainty. "You should summon him and ask."

I would have dearly loved to do precisely that, but I wasn't sure of the reception I'd receive from him. He'd made it clear the last time we met that he wished to end whatever lay between us. He'd driven the point home by not coming to me since.

A footman entered carrying a tea service on a silver tray. I watched as he deposited cups, saucers, teapot, and other pieces on the table. A lull snuffed out the conversations and

I looked up to see everyone watching me. I cast my audience a genteel smile and rose.

"Celia, shall we?"

"Let me gather my things." Celia liked to linger at afternoon séances, especially if our hostess was one of Society's leading ladies. I used to think it was because she enjoyed the sandwiches and buns, but now I knew it was because she wanted to make contacts among London's elite. The fact she did not wish to stay and chat to Lady Willoughby and her guests meant she knew something was wrong and wished to question me.

I sighed. Celia's interrogations were little better than her lectures and always tested my endurance.

Adelaide put a gentle hand on my arm, staying me. There was a gleam in her blue eyes and a flush to her cheeks that wasn't there before. "I wanted to ask you about my coming out ball."

"Celia and I will both be there," I said, cheering a little at the thought. "Did you not get our reply?"

"Oh, yes! We did. I'm so pleased you can come."

"Then what is it? If you need advice on gowns then I'm afraid I'm not the best person to ask." Celia and I could ill afford a new outfit each for the ball, and she had decided I alone would receive one while she wore something older. We'd relied on the dressmaker to advise us of the latest in evening fashions as we had so little experience. People like us were never invited to balls. Ever.

"I have not received an answer from George and the ball is only five days away." She shot a glance at her mother, conversing with Lady Willoughby and an elderly woman with a black veil covering her eyes. "Do you think he'll come?"

"I didn't know George's presence was so important to you."

"Oh. It is. Of course it is. I want all my friends there." She fiddled with a lock of hair at her temple, but it wasn't out of place. It never was. Adelaide had perfect hair, unlike mine, which was coal black and as messy as a child's scribble when I let it loose from its tight arrangement.

"I'm glad you consider George a friend after such a short acquaintance. He's a good man." I'd met George Culvert only recently, but already we were as close as two friends of the opposite sex could be without taking the relationship further. He was an acquaintance of Jacob's and a demonologist with an extensive library on supernatural subjects. It was thanks to his books and his help that Jacob and I had stopped demons and evil spirits from overrunning London.

"He is," Adelaide said quietly. "The best." She blushed again.

"Have you developed feelings for him?" Perhaps it was a little too direct, but I wasn't fond of dancing around important subjects. And what could be more important than the hearts of two dear friends?

Adelaide's blush deepened and she lowered her head but not before I saw her cast another glance at her mother. "The Culverts are not the sort of family of which we approve." It was such an odd thing for her to say that I wondered if she were merely repeating words uttered by her parents. Although George was wealthy, his mother was a social-climbing, small-minded woman, and the late Mr. Culvert had been an eccentric with an interest in the supernatural, like George himself. I could not see the cynical and upright Lord Preston sitting down to dine with a demonologist. Which was why Adelaide's invitation to George had been such a surprise. Her invitation to me was even more extraordinary. Her father didn't like me. He'd called me a fraud to my face and ordered me off his property more than once. Adelaide and her mother must have convinced him somehow, but even so, I wasn't looking forward to seeing him on the night.

"Nevertheless, George is a good man, as you say," Adelaide whispered behind her hand, as if she'd said something wicked.

I opened my mouth to question her further when a middle-aged man walked into the drawing room. Behind him, ducking a little beneath the doorway, stood Lord Preston.

Damnation.

"My dear!" cried Lady Willoughby. She jumped to her feet, knocking the table. The teacups rattled in their saucers. "You're home early."

"No one was at the club except for Preston here," said Lord Willoughby. He bowed to his wife. "My apologies, but I wasn't aware you had guests this afternoon." His friendly gap-toothed smile was bestowed to each of the ladies in turn. Until he got to me. It slipped right off his face. "Er...I don't believe we've had the pleasure."

Lady Willoughby looked like an insect frozen in a block of ice. Her large eyes bulged, accentuating the thinness of her face and long neck. "Oh, uh, yes. This is Miss Emily Chambers and her sister, Miss Celia Chambers."

"You!" Lord Preston stepped forward, looking like a thundercloud about to ruin a picnic. "What are *you* doing here?"

"We were just leaving." I didn't want an ugly confrontation with him, not in front of women we wanted— needed—as our customers, and not while Lady Preston and Adelaide were present. It would only humiliate them. Something that Lord Preston seemed to care little about.

Adelaide made a small, wheezing sound of misery, but her mother was all action. She moved smoothly to Lord Preston's side and clasped his arm. "What a lovely surprise," she said, situating herself between her husband and me. It didn't do any good. He simply glared at me over the top of her head. "This is a fortuitous meeting," she went on in her placating voice. "You can escort us home. Perhaps we'll send the carriage ahead and we all three can walk. It's not far and the day is pleasant."

Lord Preston blinked. He looked down at his wife and his expression softened. It was only then that I noticed the whiteness of Lady Preston's knuckles as they gripped his arm. He couldn't fail to have felt her fingers through his coat sleeve.

Celia looped her arm through mine and hustled me toward our hostess. "Thank you for your kind invitation," she said as if they were old friends and we had not come to conduct business. Trade of any sort was frowned upon by Upper Society. People should not be seen to earn money, or heard to talk about working for a living. Work was vulgar, coarse, something only the middle and lower classes needed to do. I didn't think we could afford to worry about such niceties, but Celia thought otherwise. She didn't ask Lady Willoughby about payment, nor did she sell our services to any of the other ladies present. It was as if we'd simply stopped by for afternoon tea.

"I'm sorry Lord Fulham couldn't oblige us by staying longer," I said. I felt Celia twitch beside me. So be it. I wanted to give Lady Willoughby an explanation for her father's all-too-brief visit. Whether she believed me or not, I couldn't say, although her polite smile did seem a little pained. "Sometimes it happens. The spirit world is unpredictable."

Lord Preston muttered something from the doorway. It was probably just as well that I couldn't hear him because it mustn't have been kind if Lady Preston's tight-lipped expression was anything to go by. She tugged her husband aside so that we could leave the drawing room. I didn't want to pass him, but I had no choice.

"Goodbye, Adelaide," I said to my friend.

She gave me a reassuring smile, which I returned to the best of my ability. Then I was alongside Lord and Lady Preston. Despite Celia's attempt to drag me past, I paused. And beamed.

"Thank you, Lady Preston," I said. "It's been lovely to see you again."

"And you, Miss Chambers. You and your sister are always welcome at our house."

I won't deny that it felt good to see Lord Preston's face turn a deep shade of violet. He did manage not to splutter his outrage and retract his wife's offer, which must have taken a great deal of effort.

"We shall see you at the ball," Lady Preston went on.

Lord Preston grunted but held his tongue.

Celia finally drew me forward and we were met outside the drawing room by the butler. He escorted us to the front door and paid Celia the amount due for the séance.

"I thought Lord Preston was going to argue with you right in front of everyone," she said once we were on the pavement out the front of the Willoughbys' townhouse.

"I thought his head was going to explode." I laughed. I was feeling reckless and ridiculous all of a sudden. Surviving a battle with Lord Preston always did that to me, and I had not only survived on this occasion, I had won.

We walked through the exclusive area of Belgravia, past tall, slender buildings and along streets swept clean of mud and horse dung. But not even Belgravia could escape London's soot. It dusted front porch steps and window shutters, nestled into the grooves between bricks, and threw a veil across the sky, shielding us from the sun.

"It seems Lord Preston knows we're going to Adelaide's ball," I said, sobering. "I was a little afraid that we'd turn up on the night and he'd throw us out."

"You thought Lady Preston hadn't discussed it with him first?" Celia scoffed. "Of course she had. She wouldn't invite anyone against her husband's wishes."

"I suppose not." I had assumed my invitation was sent before he was shown the guest list to ensure it couldn't be retracted. George's invitation too. "But why would he agree to have me there when he can't bear the sight of me?"

"Because it's obviously important to Adelaide," Celia said. "He wants to make her happy. She is his only surviving child after all."

I stopped and stared at her. She stopped too. "What is it?" she asked.

"You amaze me sometimes, Celia. That was quite an astute observation."

"You don't have the monopoly on cleverness in this family, you know."

I couldn't think of any response that wouldn't offend her so I continued walking. "I admit that I had assumed Lord Preston wouldn't care about Adelaide's wishes."

"On some things, perhaps not, but on this matter it seems he does. His wife's wishes too, of course."

That lulled me into a thoughtful silence. Perhaps Lord Preston wasn't the tyrant I'd originally pegged him to be.

"Did Lord Fulham's spirit say anything to you?" Celia asked, stopping at the intersection with busy Sloane Street. "From the look on your face, I'd say he did and that it wasn't something you liked hearing. He didn't insult you, did he?"

"No. He appeared much faded and very weak."

"As with Madame Friage yesterday."

I'd told Celia my concerns following our last séance, but both of us had dismissed Madame Friage's faintness at the time. We'd assumed she was about to crossover from the Waiting Area to the Otherworld, but now Lord Fulham had appeared just as faded, and he had said he was not going to cross. That he *could* not, and nor could the other spirits.

The steady stream of omnibuses and coaches meant we had to concentrate as we crossed Sloane Street and neither of us spoke until we reached the other side.

I rounded on Celia as she shook her skirt to dislodge some of the street grime that had dared cling to its hem. "I'm worried," I said. "Something is wrong in the Waiting Area."

"It would appear so."

"We must do something. I should summon J—"

"No! You will not summon him. We can work around this little problem without him."

Work around? Little problem? "Celia, what are you talking about? This is a potential disaster, not only for the poor spirits who can't cross, but for our business too. If word gets out that ghosts aren't co-operating, then our bookings will dry up. I can't conduct a séance without ghosts." If anything would propel Celia into action it would be the mention of our income dwindling.

"You could pretend the spirits are present."

"Celia!" I could no more act my way through an entire séance than I could perform on a stage in front of hundreds of people. The latter had been another of Celia's wild schemes only the week before, one I'd refused to participate in.

"It may be the only way." She clutched my hand and looked at me with an expression that hardened her pretty features and wrinkled her otherwise smooth brow. "Emily, we cannot afford to lose any customers."

A carriage rolled up and the window was pushed down by a hand clad in a brown leather glove. Lord Preston's hand, going by the family's coat of arms on the carriage door.

The first voice I heard was not Lord Preston's, however, but his wife's. "Please, leave her be, Reginald. There's no need to create a scene."

Celia took my arm. The sharp talons of her fingers pierced through the layers of my clothing. "Is there something we can do for you, my lord?" she asked coolly.

Lord Preston's face appeared through the window, his tall hat skimming the top of the frame. He was handsome, for an older man, but his prominent brow made him look angry all the time. Or perhaps being angry all of the time was what had made his brow so pronounced in the first place.

"Do not think I've given up," he snarled. "Do not think you've gotten away with anything, Miss Chambers. You are a fraud. Your tricks are heartless and cruel and I *will* discredit you."

Celia took a step back as if he'd pushed her, but I stood my ground, even as she tried to pull me away from the coach. I would not give into him. I was many things—a fatherless bastard of African descent, a woman of trade, and a magnet for trouble—but I was *not* a fraud.

"Is that all, my lord?" I asked with the sweetest voice I could muster through my seething anger. "Because I'm very busy and there's a ghost over there who wishes to speak to me." It was a lie, but it made him look in the direction of my nod, which I found perversely amusing.

"Reginald, please," came Lady Preston's pleading voice from within the carriage. "Let's go. For Adelaide's sake."

I thought I heard sniffing, but I could have been mistaken. The rumbling of dozens of wheels and *clip clop* of horses' hooves along Sloane Street was enough to drown out most small sounds.

"Cease your fraudulent act, Miss Chambers," Lord Preston said, his voice lowered enough that I could still hear it but probably not his wife and daughter behind him. "For their sakes, if not for your own." He withdrew into the cabin and pulled up the window with a violent shove. The coach rolled away and joined the traffic.

I stared after it. My heart kicked violently inside my chest as if it were restarting after having ceased. My hands began to shake and I clasped them tightly together so that Celia didn't notice.

"What a rude, horrid man," she said. "Pay him no mind. His words are just that, words. As long as he doesn't repeat them at the ball, all will be well, and I do believe he'll keep his opinions to himself that night."

I hoped she was right. He might be prepared to discredit me in front of his family, but he had refrained in public so far. That wasn't to say he wouldn't have a few private, quiet words with his friends over dinner. I wouldn't put anything past Lord Preston when it came to smearing my reputation.

"It dumbfounds me that a father would say such things to his daughter's friend," I said.

"Not even if he thought he was right?" Celia asked, steering me down the pavement. "Perhaps he thinks he's protecting her from further hurt. She and her mother have suffered greatly from Jacob's death, and if he truly believes you are indeed a fraud, he would not want you hurting them further with what he thinks are lies."

Sometimes I hated it when she made sense. "Stop making

12

excuses for him, Celia. He's awful and that's that."

"His manners could certainly do with some improving. Whoever said the upper classes were the most polite got it wrong. In my opinion, they are the most ill-mannered."

We walked side by side past shops and distinctive red brick houses until we reached Druids Way. I planted my hand on my hat to stop it being blown off in the sudden breeze that always greeted us in our street. Celia had a ribbon beneath her chin keeping her bonnet securely in place so that she could continue to hold my arm and carry the carpet bag.

With my head bent into the wind, I didn't see the spirit until we reached the steps leading up to our front door. He was sitting on the top step, his forehead resting on arms crossed over his knees. I couldn't see his face, but I didn't need to. I knew who it was, even though the difference in him was profound.

"Jacob!"

He lifted his head and I was struck by the weariness that shadowed his eyes. His shoulders were stooped, as if they carried a load too heavy to bear. "Em."

I pulled free of Celia and ran to him. "What's happened?" I squatted before him and touched his cheek. It was cooler than usual. "You're so faint." Despite Madame Friage and Lord Fulham both appearing extremely faded, I hadn't thought Jacob would suffer the same fate. He was more solid than every other spirit I'd encountered. Whereas they were smudged at the edges, he was as sharp and bold to me as any live person.

Not anymore. Whatever had befallen them affected Jacob as well. Which meant he was struggling to remain in our realm.

Jacob closed his hand over mine. It didn't feel as solid as usual, and that scared me. "I'm growing fainter because I'm dying, Em."

"But you're already dead."

He gave me a crooked smile. "Yes, but not like this. This is different. If I continue to fade, I'll no longer exist as a conscious entity. None of us will."

No. It wasn't possible. There must be some horrible mistake. But Jacob didn't look like a man in error. He closed his eyes and tipped his head forward onto his knees again.

Oh God.

"What's he saying?" Celia asked.

My throat tightened, but I managed to speak, albeit softly. "He says he, and all the spirits in the Waiting Area, are going to become nothing."

CHAPTER 2

"This requires a cup of tea," Celia announced. "Let's go inside."

"I don't think tea will solve my problem," Jacob said.

I didn't think so either, but it would make Celia feel better and remove us from prying eyes. Our elderly neighbors liked to occupy their day by watching the street through their windows.

Lucy, our maid, met us in the hallway. I told her Jacob was present and she went very still. Only her eyeballs moved, scanning the vicinity. She could not see him, of course. Only I could, and Cara, my ten year-old aunt who'd moved into the spare bedroom.

"Where's Cara?" I asked, hanging up my hat on the coat stand.

"In the kitchen helping me bake." Lucy took the bag Celia passed to her. "Shall I fetch her, miss?"

"No!" Celia and I both said together. I didn't want Cara to worry or feel that she needed to help us. She'd had a difficult life and it was time she enjoyed the few years of childhood remaining and leave serious matters to her elders. Apparently Celia had the same idea.

"Can you bring tea into the drawing room, please?" Celia

said.

"Yes, Miss Chambers." Lucy turned to go but stopped. "Oh, I almost forgot. A man called today." Her gaze flicked to me, so naturally I asked if the visitor were George.

"Or Mr. Hyde?" Celia asked. She was referring to Theodore Hyde, a gentleman who'd been calling on me frequently of late.

My face grew hot and I didn't dare look at Jacob. He wanted me to encourage Theo's attentions, despite the intense, unresolved feelings between himself and me. He wanted me to live a full life until we met again in the Otherworld, but I was still unsure of my feelings toward Theo. I liked him very much, but did I love him enough to consider marrying him? Perhaps, in time...

"Not Mr. Hyde or Mr. Culvert neither," Lucy said. "It was a stranger." She bit on her plump bottom lip and her gaze once more settled on me.

"Did he leave his name?" Celia asked.

"No, Miss Chambers."

"Did he state his business?" I said.

"No, Miss Emily. He said he'd return another time."

"How odd." We had no more questions and Celia dismissed Lucy. The maid bobbed a curtsy and bustled back to the kitchen.

"It's the height of rudeness not to leave a calling card," Celia muttered as she walked into the drawing room. "The absolute height." She paused in the doorway and sighed at the threadbare sofa before proceeding to it. We'd almost bought a new one, but she had declared my ball gown more important. An investment in my future, she'd called it. Most of the profits from our séances had been used to pay for the dress.

"Jacob, please sit," I urged him when he stood next to the fireplace, his customary position when he came to visit. "Save your energy."

He looked like he would refuse, but then he gave a single nod and collapsed into the nearby armchair as if his legs could no longer hold him upright. Celia seemed to relax a little as she always did when she knew precisely where he was in the room. She must have seen the indentation he made in the upholstery.

I touched his shoulder to reassure myself that he was still solid enough for me to *feel* him. He was so faint, so unlike himself, that I feared my hand would go straight through him, as it would if I wasn't a medium. Luckily, I could still feel him, but he was so cold.

My face must have shown my worry because he said, "I'm all right, Em."

I grazed my knuckles along his jaw, down his neck to the collar of his shirt.

Celia cleared her throat. "Tell us what's happening up there. Our last two séances have not gone according to plan and Emily said there's something wrong in the Waiting Area."

He edged away from my hand, as if he couldn't bear my touch.

"Come sit with me, Emily," Celia ordered.

I obeyed, backing away from Jacob without taking my gaze off him. He kept his on me too and there was a longing in their depths that punched through to my heart. I'd missed the way he looked at me—like I was a balm for deep wounds. A shiver of desire rippled across my skin, caressing me like a warm breeze.

He looked away suddenly and stared into the unlit grate. "The Waiting Area is in chaos."

"Chaos?" I echoed. "What do you mean?"

"Spirits are disappearing and not reappearing and no one knows where they've gone. They simply...fade away into nothingness. Few are able to come here at will anymore, and those who can are unable to stay."

"We know." I told him what Madame Friage and Lord Fulham had said.

"I am the strongest spirit," he said, "the most...physical for want of a better word."

"You always were."

"Some would say I was an overachiever in life and continue to be so in death."

It sounded silly, but it was no laughing matter, particularly the part about when he was alive. From the information we'd gathered, his murder was linked closely to the type of person he'd been—somewhat self-absorbed and yes, overachieving. His admission cut to the bone and the pain of it was imprinted clear on his face.

"Everyone is afraid," he went on. "No one seems to know what to do. So I've been sent by the Administrators to ask for your help, Emily."

"Oh." I thought he'd come because he wanted to see me. Or to say goodbye. I gulped back hot tears.

"What does he want?" Celia's brisk tone set me on edge even more. She was extremely protective of me and disliked having me exposed to danger. It usually led to a great many lies on my part, something I disliked but found utterly necessary if I were to get anything done. "You must tell me," she said when I hesitated.

I told her what Jacob had said. "But what can Emily do?" she said, her tone more subdued than I expected.

Jacob's presence flared for a moment then dimmed alarmingly.

"Jacob!"

"I'm here," he said as he returned. He sighed. "Tell your sister..." He shook his head. "I was about to say, tell her not to worry. But I cannot lie to either of you. If past events are any indication, there will be danger involved."

"Yes," I said quietly, "I'm sure there will be." But there was no way I would tell Celia that in such plain terms.

"I don't like it, Em," he said. "I don't like asking this of you."

"But you have no choice," I finished for him.

"There is always a choice." He lowered his head into his hands and dragged his fingers through his dark hair. "I could have chosen to do nothing while all those spirits in the

Waiting Area fade into non-existence."

"Including yourself."

He rubbed his hand across the back of his neck and groaned. "Or I could ask you or Cara for help." He laughed, low and bitter.

"Thank you," I whispered. "You made the right decision." It would seem he thought as we did—that Cara was too young to bear such a burden on her small shoulders—but I don't think the decision was made lightly. Jacob had an aversion to putting me in danger too.

"Then why do I feel so wretched?" He stood suddenly and his presence solidified.

"Your anger suits you," I said, trying to lighten the tone of our conversation.

"I'm not angry," he muttered, turning away from me to stare into the fireplace.

"Emily," Celia said. "Tell me this instant what is being discussed. I will not be ignored."

"Celia, ignoring you is an impossibility."

She looked down at her skirts and made a show of smoothing them.

"I'm sorry," I said, closing my hand over hers. "I didn't mean to sound so horrid."

"I know. Now stop avoiding the topic and tell me what Jacob said. I am on pins and needles."

"He said not to worry." I studiously kept my gaze from wandering to Jacob as he turned to regard me, both brows raised. I could not lie if he challenged me, even if he did so silently. "He wants me to conduct some research in George's library to find out why the spirits are disappearing. So it looks like George and I will be afflicted with nothing more dangerous than paper cuts."

She gave me a small smile of relief. "Excellent. Research in the library. You and George are very good at that."

"You, Emily Chambers, are devious." Jacob shook his head and chuckled. My heart flooded. I wanted to see him laugh more often. I suspected cheerfulness was his natural state, or at least it had been when he was alive, but his death had darkened his soul.

Being murdered can do that to a person.

Finding his murderer had been one of the few things to keep me occupied in his absence these last two weeks, but it had been a frustrating endeavor. Lady Preston had informed me just prior to our séance earlier that the only boy named Frederick in Jacob's year at Oxford to have died was a Frederick Seymour, and that he had indeed killed himself. It merely confirmed what we'd already learned and it left us no closer to discovering the truth behind Jacob's murder. Jacob remembered his murderer blaming him for Frederick's death, but how could he be responsible? They may have fought, but Jacob hadn't killed him. Frederick had got up and run away afterward. And Jacob could hardly be held responsible for the suicide of someone he barely knew.

Discovering the truth had become as important to me as discovering the identity of my own father. He and his family needed closure, to move on. Once we found his killer, we would find Jacob's body. Lord and Lady Preston would be able to finally bury their son and see justice served. I suspected it would also allow Jacob's spirit to crossover and be at peace. It's what I wanted second most in all the world. Foremost, I wanted to be with him...someday.

Although it seemed crossing over to the Otherworld was looking increasingly doubtful for *all* ghosts, not just Jacob.

"I think you need to tell me more," I said to him. "So that George and I know what to look for," I added for Celia's benefit.

"And that nice Mr. Hyde too," she said. "I'm sure he'll enjoy researching alongside you both in the library.

Jacob stiffened and stared hard at the fireplace.

"Theo is very busy," I said. "He has his legal studies and is working in a law office three afternoons a week." Theo might be a gentleman, but he was as poor as me. Well, perhaps not quite *that* poor, but he wasn't well-to-do like his rich and titled relatives. He needed to work for a living. Celia thought a lawyer was a decidedly good prospect for me, and I had to agree that a girl in my position couldn't hope for better.

"That may be so," she said, "but he seems to find the time to visit us often." The triumphant lift of her chin was most certainly for Jacob's benefit. She didn't dislike him. She just didn't think he was a good influence on me. Looking at it from her perspective, I could see why. Being in love with a ghost was not something I would wish on anyone. Our future together depended upon my death.

But I had no choice in the matter. The heart will feel what the heart will feel.

"Go on, Jacob," I urged him. "Tell me what to look for."

He collapsed into the armchair once again. "The Administrators believe the Waiting Area is being sabotaged."

"Sabotaged! By whom?"

"And why?" asked Celia.

"And how?"

"I cannot tell you how," he said. "The Administrators haven't discovered the method. They've been too busy trying to keep the weakest spirits within the Waiting Area. As to the whom and the why..." His exhausted gaze locked with mine. "We think it's the same person who brought the demon to this realm and summoned the spirit of Mortlock." Mortlock was the vicious ghost who'd possessed Adelaide and then George.

"Your killer," I said on a breath.

Jacob nodded. "He was trying to hurt me through you and my family, but I think he has a new tactic—destroy me directly. I can't pretend I'm not glad," he said quietly. "All I ever wanted was for my loved ones to be safe."

My insides melted. To be classed alongside his family was an honor. To be called a loved one was a dream come true. "Perhaps he somehow knows you haven't been here and thought you no longer cared for me."

"Or perhaps he saw Hyde visiting frequently and decided *you* no longer cared for *me*." His voice was dark but gave no indication of what he thought of the matter. Considering he was the one pushing me in Theo's direction, I would think he was happy with this unexpected benefit.

"Your scenario does seem more likely since he cannot see you," I said.

"His murderer is doing this?" Celia frowned. I could see she was trying very hard to keep up with the conversation despite only hearing half of it. "It does seem likely after all the trouble he's caused so far."

"Or she," I said. "The murderer may be a woman."

"True. Whomever it is, they have a great deal of knowledge about the supernatural."

"Someone from the Society for Supernatural Activity perhaps."

"You're thinking of Price?" He shook his head. "I'm not sure if anyone in the Society is that knowledgeable. They're mostly a group of men and women with an interest in demons, ghosts, and inexplicable phenomena. The knowledge required to do this is obscure and beyond a little dabbling in the supernatural."

"Price might have gained that knowledge from another source."

"So might anyone else."

"Not that you are going to confront this Mr. Price," Celia said. "I absolutely forbid you to go anywhere near him. Do you understand me, Emily?"

"Of course," I said. "I wouldn't do anything so stupid."

Celia huffed.

Jacob narrowed his eyes. "For once I agree with her. Do not do anything yet except go through the books in George's library. If you can't find something there, we'll have to wait for the Administrators to guide me when they're ready."

I expected Jacob to disappear to conserve his energy, but he remained, watching me intently. It was unnerving but exhilarating at the same time. He was the most handsome man I knew, his features strong and defined. There were no weak lines on his face or in the set of his broad shoulders.

He wore only the shirt and trousers he'd died in, and I couldn't stop my gaze wandering to the gap where his shirt opened at his chest. I wanted to kiss him there, feel the smooth skin and tease a sigh from his lips.

He suddenly faded again and I opened my mouth to call him, but he returned.

"Are you all right?" My heart pulsed in my throat and I swear I could hear the clang my nerves made as they jangled.

He nodded. "Emily, do you recall that I said I would look for your father in New South Wales?"

I waved my hand in dismissal. "Never mind that now. There are more important things to be done first."

"Your situation is important too, Em."

"Thank you." I gave him a grim smile. "But it can wait. Besides, you may not be able to travel so far in this state."

"When this is over, and if I am able, I *will* find him for you."

"You won't need to go anywhere," said Cara from the doorway. My ten-year-old aunt nodded a greeting at Jacob as she came into the drawing room carrying a plate of almond biscuits. She was a medium, like me, the ability to communicate with spirits having been passed down to us from our distant African ancestors. She looked pretty with her dark wavy hair tied up with blue ribbons. She wore a matching blue dress that used to be mine, but Celia had pulled it out of the attic and given it to Cara when she came to live with us.

"What do you mean?" I asked her.

"He's here in London."

"My father? Your brother?"

"I seen him," Cara said, setting the plate on the table.

I waited for Celia to correct her sentence, but she didn't. My sister must have been shocked into stupidity by Cara's announcement. One glance at her proved otherwise, however. She sat primly on the edge of the sofa, her gaze upon her hands in her lap. It was only on closer inspection that I noticed them shaking.

"He came here while you were out," Cara said. "Lucy let him in and I watched them talking. He didn't see me."

"Do you mean the man who didn't leave his name or calling card?" I asked.

"He looked like us," she said, her serious eyes fixed on me. "Only a little bit darker."

No wonder Lucy had been eyeing me surreptitiously when she said a man had come calling. She must have suspected he was my kin but had not wanted to broach the subject of our similarity, or had not known how to do so politely.

"Did he say anything else?" I pressed Cara. "Did he mention where he is staying?"

She shook her head. "He asked if Mrs. Chambers and Miss Celia Chambers still lived here. Lucy told him Mrs. Chambers was dead and you two were out. Then he left."

"What was his reaction to the news of our mother's death?" I asked. "Did he seem upset?"

She shrugged one shoulder.

"I wonder why he came back from New South Wales." It was all so surreal, so fantastical, that I couldn't quite take it in. My father, Louis, was back and he'd come looking for us. We thought he'd made a new life for himself in that far-off land and didn't want past relationships to interfere with it. That's what Louis' father, my grandfather, had told us. Since Mama and Celia never heard from him again, we'd assumed old Mr. Moreau spoke the truth.

"Tea," said Celia. The single, decisive word punctured my thoughts. "Where's Lucy? We must have our tea."

I caught Jacob watching me, his finger slowly stroking his lips. "Are you all right?" he asked.

"I think so. My grandfather will probably know where he is." I rose, but Celia pulled me back down onto the sofa with a hard jerk.

"You are not going anywhere," she snapped. "And you are certainly not going to see that madman."

"But my father—"

"No! If Louis wishes to visit us, then let him come." She smoothed down her skirts, so it was difficult to see if her hands still shook. "We will not go chasing him around the city. Understand?"

"Yes, Celia."

She squeezed my arm then rose and left the drawing room muttering about tea.

Jacob sighed. "You're going to visit your grandfather, aren't you?"

I nodded. "Of course."

"Good," said Cara. "I'll come too. I don't like being left out." She arched her eyebrows at me then at Jacob, a childishly defiant gleam in her eyes.

I sighed. "How much did you hear?"

"Everything."

The defiance vanished and she knelt on the floor in front of me. She clasped my hands. "You can trust me, Emily. I want to help."

"And you will," I said to placate her.

"Indeed," Jacob muttered. "We may need all the help we can get."

CHAPTER 3

I couldn't get away from the house without Celia noticing until the following day. When she went shopping early the next morning, Cara and I slipped out. My aunt insisted on coming with me. I didn't see the harm in allowing her, and it was nice to have company. We caught the omnibus to the Leather Lane market where François Moreau kept a stall selling fruit and vegetables. It was easy to spot the faded red awning over his cart next to the lamp seller, despite the crowds.

I wasn't looking forward to seeing my grandfather again. He had a tendency to laugh like a madman, which I suppose he was. Getting straight answers out of him had proved difficult so far.

"Have you seen him?" I asked Moreau after we explained the reason for our visit.

"My boy?" he said with a lilting French accent. "Bah! He's a fool, that one." He rearranged the onions in their display box on his cart but not for any discernible reason that I could see except to keep his hands busy. The new pattern looked exactly like the old one. "*Imbécile.*"

"Papa, you do know that he's back, don't you?" asked Cara.

"He went to New South Wales. Long, long way away."

"Yes, but he returned," I said, trying very hard to keep the note of impatience out of my voice. "Has he been to see you?"

François didn't look up as he swapped onions with onions, over and over again, his brown hands fast and nimble. "He went to New South Wales. Better there for people like him. People like us." His fingers suddenly stilled and he clenched an onion in his fist. His head jerked up and his pitch-black gaze drilled into me. "Go! Now! Leave Louis be. He is my only son."

"But Papa," Cara begged, "tell us where to find him. He is my brother and Emily's father."

François shook the onion at her. "Go away! You not my daughter no more. You be with them now. They trouble," he muttered. "Girls always bring trouble."

I clasped Cara's hand and drew her away from my grandfather, her father. It was a mistake to come to the market. We weren't going to get answers from him. We would simply have to wait for Louis to come to us. He had once, hopefully he would again.

"How did you live with him for as long as you did?" I asked Cara as we wended our way through the stalls selling everything from eels to hair combs, sherbet to Dutch dolls.

"We didn't talk much. He brought home food and I kept out of his way. He wasn't like a real father. He didn't even know about me until I was eight."

That she could speak so calmly about her father's disregard amazed me. He had not asked her how she fared with us, people who'd been complete strangers to her mere weeks ago. Then again, Cara was quite detached. Her eyes lit up at all the usual things, like new clothes or toys or a plate full of cakes, but when it came to more serious emotions, she seemed incapable of feeling anything.

I took her hand and was surprised that it trembled. It seemed I was wrong. She *was* upset by the encounter. It amazed me that it didn't show on her face.

I squeezed her fingers and she squeezed back but neither of us spoke of François Moreau again.

We dodged the early morning shoppers and loafers and made our way up Leather Lane. Street sellers shouted over each other to catch our attention, but we ignored them. The man with shrimps poking out of his hat-band crying, "Shrimps at a penny a pint," smelled particularly foul. We gave him the widest berth of all.

"I must get to George's," I said, hurrying Cara through the maze. "I'll see you home safely first."

"I can go on my own."

"I know, but I would be a terrible niece if I allowed my aunt to roam the streets unattended."

She giggled and I grinned. We both saw the absurdity of an aunt being seven years younger than the niece.

"Are you going to look through Mr. Culvert's books to find out why Mr. Beaufort is fading in and out?" she asked when her giggles subsided.

"Yes." It was nice not to be the only one able to see and hear spirits anymore, even though it meant I couldn't have secret conversations with Jacob when she was near. Cara's very existence made me feel less of a freak.

As luck would have it, an omnibus was letting off passengers and continuing in our direction. It had seats inside where it was warmer than riding on top, and I informed the conductor we wished to travel as far as Chelsea.

"Can I help you and Mr. Culvert?" Cara asked as we took our seats.

"Not yet," I said. "But I'll be sure to let you know if there's something you can do."

"Good. I don't like being left out. I *am* ten, you know, not a baby."

***

I made sure Cara arrived home safely, then I set off again before Celia could stop me. No doubt Cara would tell her where we'd been and I would get a lecture about my disobedience later. So be it.

George was just stepping out of his carriage when I strolled up to his Wilton Crescent house. "Emily!" he said, beaming. "What a lovely surprise." Then he suddenly frowned. "Or is it? You look a little anxious."

"I am." I decided not to tell him about my father's return. That could wait until after I'd spoken to Louis and learned of his plans. Besides, there were more troubling matters to address. "Something's happened in the Waiting Area. If I'd known you were going to be out and about early I would have come straight after breakfast. I thought you might sleep late." The Belgravia set often didn't rise until late in the morning, or so I'd been told. I regretted losing valuable time that could have been better spent researching and not chasing my elusive father.

"You can visit in the middle of the night if it's important." He opened the front door and a footman sailed across the tiles to meet us. "Library?" George said to me as the footman took our coats and hats.

"Most definitely."

"Greggs, have tea sent up to the library and lunch in an hour. Is Mother at home?"

"Mrs. Culvert is preparing to go out, sir," Greggs said in his deadpan voice.

"Preparing, eh? That could take hours." George hooked his arm through mine. "There's no need to tell her that I have a guest in the library. Unless she asks of course, then I suppose you must answer truthfully."

"Very good, sir."

"You could order him to lie to her," I whispered as we walked arm in arm into the library adjoining the entrance hall. "He is your servant after all, not your mother's."

"Mother has Greggs wrapped around her little finger. Besides, she would sniff out the presence of a visitor, particularly one connected to Lady Preston, regardless of what I tell her. Mother's senses function all too well when hunting prey that could help her in certain circles. You, my dear, are a tasty morsel indeed."

I stopped at the massive central table with its leather inlay and squat, solid legs, and set my reticule on the surface. "I'm not connected to Lady Preston at all. We are merely acquaintances."

"But you are friends with Adelaide, aren't you? I mean, Miss Beaufort." From the way he leaned forward, I sensed he was interested in the answer for his own sake, not his mother's.

"We are friends of sorts, although I'm not sure how close we are considering she is the daughter of an earl and I am the illegitimate daughter of a—" I realized I didn't know what my father did for a living. Perhaps he was a grocer like his father. "A nobody."

He winced. "Friendship knows no boundaries, Emily. Nor does love."

"You are sounding positively egalitarian, George." I scanned one of the floor-to-ceiling bookshelves that occupied three entire walls of the cavernous room. George's library was very impressive, with many of the books being old and rare. His library was a reader's dream, as long as that reader had an interest in the paranormal. "What's happened to make you so fair-minded? When we first met, you thought my friendship with Adelaide quite shocking."

"You happened, as a matter of fact."

"Me?" I paused, my hand on a book spine, and looked at him over my shoulder.

"Yes, you. Your friendship has enriched me beyond anything these dusty books ever taught me." He swept his arms wide to indicate the library with its thousands upon thousands of volumes.

"Why George, you're being very sweet all of a sudden." I narrowed my eyes. "Do you want something from me?" His cheeks reddened and I laughed. "I knew it!"

"No, no. Oh very well, yes." He gave me a crooked smile and pushed his glasses up his nose. "I simply want to ask you some questions about Miss Beaufort. What sort of dances she likes best, her hobbies, that sort of thing."

Meaning he wanted to charm her at the ball. Dear George got sweeter and sweeter with every moment. "What I could teach you about women in general, and Adelaide in particular, would take the rest of the day, and that's only because you know so little. I'm sorry, George, we don't have the luxury today."

He sighed. "Of course. You did say it was important. Something's happened in the Waiting Area?"

I told him about the fading spirits and everything Jacob had said. "He's going to find out what he can from the Administrators, but it's chaotic up there apparently."

"And he thinks a living person is causing the chaos?"

"He does. But how can that be? How can someone from here influence what happens there?"

"A curse perhaps." He moved one of the ladders fixed to the bookshelf railing and positioned it near the fireplace. That corner of the library seemed gloomier than the rest, being furthest away from the large arched windows that looked out upon Wilton Crescent.

"It seems likely since our recent problems with demons and possessions have mostly come about from curses in one form or another."

Some curses, or incantations, could only be spoken by a medium for them to work, and some needed a talisman or object, but others could be uttered by anyone. Learning the words, however, was another issue entirely.

"George," I hedged, "you may not like what I'm going to suggest, but do you think someone from the Society For Supernatural Activity would have the know-how to do something like this?"

He looked down at me from halfway up the ladder. "Someone like Price you mean?"

"Yes." Leviticus Price was an eccentric scholar connected to the man who'd released the shape-shifting demon. He'd also proved evasive when we tried to ask him about possession. I didn't like him. He made feel like I was little better than something he'd scraped off the bottom of his shoe. Perhaps I was biased by my dislike and forming unfair conclusions, but so be it. We had to start somewhere.

"It's possible." George tilted his head to the side to read the book spines. "But I have the most extensive library of all the members and he hasn't been here. Nor has anyone else of late and I doubt our villain would find a text on ways to disrupt the Otherworld anywhere else in London."

"Perhaps he hasn't found the information in a book at all."

George peered down his nose at me. "Where else would he find it? Who would be in possession of such obscure knowledge and not write it down?"

I shrugged, but the more I thought about it, the more the idea took flight. All the books in George's library were written in the last few centuries by Englishmen or translated into English from foreign texts, but the authors must have gotten the information from somewhere. So where? Who had told them about the supernatural in the first place?

"He was elected Grand Master, you know," George said, flicking through a heavy leather bound book.

"Price? Grand Master of what?"

"The Grand Master is head of the Society." He shut the book, tucked it under his arm, and descended the ladder. "I'm not sure how he managed it. He's not particularly well liked, but he is extremely clever. Perhaps the general membership thought he deserved to be leader since he's so devoted to the supernatural."

"Does it give him any special powers?"

"Like flying or super-human strength?"

"Very amusing."

George's blue eyes twinkled behind his glasses. "He chairs our meetings and has the final say on changes to our charter."

"That doesn't sound very interesting."

A footman entered carrying a tray with tea things. He set it down just as Mrs. Culvert entered. "Ah, Miss Chambers, what a *lovely* surprise." Her tight smile didn't reach her eyes, which were equally tight, pulled back at the corners by her severe hairstyle. "How *are* you, my dear?"

"Well, thank you."

"And your family?"

"My sister and aunt are also well," I said, although Mrs. Culvert didn't seem to be listening to my answer.

"Mother, don't you have a lunch appointment?" George asked.

"Yes, yes, all in good time. I want to chat to Miss Chambers first. *Such* a sweet girl. Just like her friend. What's her name again?"

I wasn't looking at George but I could practically hear his eyeballs rolling back in his head. "You know her name is Adelaide Beaufort," he said, "and we can both see through your poor attempt to disguise your interest."

When I first met George, he would never have spoken to his mother so boldly. I wasn't sure whether to be shocked or to cheer him. Mrs. Culvert wasn't a particularly pleasant lady. She didn't like me. When we'd first met, she didn't want me in her house at all. Clearly I was unacceptable company for her son to keep. Being a medium, dusky of skin, and not from Society, I wasn't the sort of girl she wanted near her son in case we formed an affection for one another. Fortunately it was her son's house and he enjoyed my company. It was only after she learned of my friendship with Adelaide that she accepted me.

Mrs. Culvert's smile didn't waver. It was as if it had been painted on along with the rouge on her cheeks. "I suppose you'll be at Miss Beaufort's coming out ball? I'm not going of course. I have other commitments that evening, but I'm sure you younger ones will enjoy yourselves."

"Mother," George said on a sigh, "do you *have* to?" He'd told me that his mother desperately wanted to go to the ball but had not received an invitation. I felt a twinge of sympathy for her, but only a twinge, mind.

Through the open door of the library, we could hear the

knocker bang on the front door. A moment, later the footman announced, "A Mr. Hyde."

"Who?" asked Mrs. Culvert.

"I wonder why Theo is here," I said.

"I imagine it's to see you," said George with a wink.

Theo entered and bowed to Mrs. Culvert and myself. "I hope I'm not intruding."

"Not at all." George introduced him to his mother. "She was just leaving."

"In a moment." Her fingers brushed her lips and she eyed Theo up and down with an undisguised flash of desire.

I couldn't blame her. Theo was a handsome man. He was blond like George, but that's where the similarity ended. Where George's hair was a riot of boyish curls, Theo's was thick and straight. He was broader in the chest and shoulders too. George had the lean frame and milky skin of a London scholar.

"Are you related to the Hydes of Mayfair?" Mrs. Culvert asked.

"I'm from Shropshire, madam, but I'm related to the Arbuthnots of Kensington," Theo said.

"Are the Arbuthnots peerage?"

"No."

"Oh." Her mouth flattened and her eyes turned hard and colorless once more. "Don't let me keep you young people from doing whatever it is you do in here." She headed for the door. "Give my regards to Miss Beaufort and Lady Preston, Miss Chambers. And do tell Miss Beaufort that George is *very much* looking forward to attending the ball." She waggled her fingers at me then left. Her heels clicked on the tiled entrance hall until they disappeared altogether.

George breathed a sigh of relief.

"Theo, what brings you here?" I asked.

He took my hands and kissed the back of one. "I wanted to see you. I went to your house, but your sister said you'd come here." His smile was warm and focused entirely on me. A little thrill skidded down my spine at the attention.

"You don't have lectures this morning?"

He rubbed my hands with his thumbs, his gaze intent on the small swirling motion. "No."

How odd. It was Tuesday and I was sure he had lectures every Tuesday morning. "And Carson and Kellerman didn't need you instead?" I asked, referring to the law firm where he worked.

He let go of my hands. "So many questions, Emily, you're worse than my aunt. No, I am not needed there today." He nodded at George. "How do you do, Culvert?"

George passed him a book. "Since you've not got anything better to do, want to help us research?"

"Of course. At least these books are more interesting than the legal tomes I usually study."

"Easier to understand too, eh?" said George, climbing the ladder once more.

Theo laughed and set the book on the table. I poured tea for us and it wasn't until I handed Theo his cup that I realized he'd been watching me.

"You're looking quite beautiful this morning," he said, accepting the cup.

My face heated as it always did. Theo had come calling at our Druids Way house many times since he'd helped to send the spirit of Mortlock back to the Otherworld. He was very attentive and always complimented me on my appearance. Although I liked it, I had not quite grown used to it. All my life people had stared at me or whispered about me because of either my talent as a medium or my darker than white skin. To now have nice things said about me, to be called beautiful and exotic by handsome men like Theo, George, and Jacob was quite a change. I was not yet accustomed to it. I might never be.

"Is your ball gown finished?" he asked.

"Almost." I pulled the book toward me since he hadn't opened it.

"The ball will be quite an event on the social calendar, and I'm rather looking forward to it."

"So am I. But for now, we must find out what is happening in the Waiting Area." I launched yet again into the details of our current supernatural problem. Theo listened, his expression growing more and more serious.

"I'm glad I'm available to help." He took a book from George who'd descended the ladder with an armful. Theo blew dust off the top.

"I don't think these ones have been touched since my father died," George said, sitting opposite.

We each set to our books. Lunch came and went, as did another round of tea, and the pile of books we finished studying grew higher and higher. When a footman entered and lit the cast iron gas lamps, I realized it had grown late in the day.

"I should go," I said. "Celia will be getting worried."

"I'll walk you home," Theo said, rising. "I'd take you in my carriage, but the driver is washing it today." He grinned. He didn't have a coach of his own. His cousin in Kensington did, but I'd not once seen Theo borrow it. Like me, he either walked or caught the omnibus.

"Tell him to stay on the main roads," said Jacob, flaring into existence next to me. My heart lurched in my chest. It was so good to see him again. "It's growing dark and some of the less frequented lanes will be dangerous." He faded a little before once more solidifying.

"Jacob is here," I announced. "If you're busy, Theo, then he can walk with me."

"No," Jacob said. "I want him to do it."

I raised my brows at him.

"I'm not busy," Theo said cheerfully.

Jacob crossed his arms and raised his brows right back at me. "It's settled then."

I tried not to be upset that he didn't want to escort me home. After all, being invisible to everyone but me was hardly a deterrent to thugs. I also knew he was trying to push me toward Theo. He'd stated his opinion on the matter of Theo courting me before. Stated it very clearly. He was certainly in favor of us spending more time alone together.

"My killer said I must give something up," he'd once told me. *"Something dear to me. You are dear to me."*

It was impossible to feel put out after that declaration. Jacob felt that giving me up would break the curse laid upon him at the moment of his death, and he would finally be allowed to crossover. I didn't like it, but I wanted what was best for him, and crossing over was definitely for the best. I couldn't bear to have him remain here and watch me grow old.

Besides, if I could not be escorted by Jacob then Theo was a good second choice. He was excellent company.

"You're not going to disagree with me, are you?" Jacob asked.

"Of course not. When have I ever been known to disagree with you?"

He snorted softly. "Frequently. I'm beginning to think it's your favorite pastime."

"If you said things that made perfectly good sense, I wouldn't need to disagree with you."

"Walking home with Theo doesn't make good sense? It does to me, Em. I won't be much help at the moment." His voice drifted as he spoke and he vanished completely.

"Jacob!"

He returned again, his brows knitted with anxiety. "See what I mean?"

I blew out a measured breath. "Have you learned anything from the Administrators?"

He perched on the edge of the table and flipped through the nearest book. Theo's eyes widened, but George didn't flutter an eyelash. He was used to Jacob now, and seeing objects move as if of their own free will no longer caught him unawares.

"They know how it's being done," he said gravely. "It's quite shocking. You may need to sit down."

I sat.

"What is it?" Theo asked. "What has he said?"

"Nothing yet." I nodded at Jacob. "Go on."

He closed the book. "You won't find the answers in any of these, I'm afraid. Not this time, although the villain *is* using a curse."

"We thought as much. It's definitely caused by a curse," I told George and Theo. "Why won't we find information about it in one of these books? They're riddled with all sorts of useful incantations."

"Not this one. It's ancient and few people know of its existence let alone the precise words. It's considered so dangerous that the custodians of the curse have never written it down."

"Custodians?"

"A Romany clan."

"Gypsies!"

"What about gypsies?" George asked.

"Thieves the lot of them!" Theo spat.

"Steady on," said George. "Surely not all of them are as bad as their reputation suggests."

"They are. Every single one." Theo crossed his arms. "They're taught how to pick pockets when they're barely out of the cradle and graduate to horse stealing and worse by Cara's age. A group of them camp near our farm every summer, and every summer we lose sheep from the fields and tools from the barn. One year they stole the bread right out of the kitchen."

"Brazen," muttered George.

I told them what Jacob had said about the ancient curse causing the havoc in the Waiting Area. "You said it was shocking," I said to him, "but uttering an old curse is not terribly earth-shattering."

"The manner in which it's delivered to the Waiting Area is," he said. "The Administrators had difficulty determining how it was happening because the method of its delivery is so astonishing." He shook his head. "I still cannot believe it."

"Tell me. I am in suspense."

He set his unblinking gaze on me. "The one delivering

the curse must be dead."

"Dead!"

"Who's dead?" George asked.

"Aside from the obvious." Theo indicated the book Jacob had been flicking through.

"The cursor is dead," I told them. "He or she delivered the curse into the Waiting Area by dying first. So that's that then. The villain is dead and most likely somewhere in the Waiting Area right now. Goodness knows why they would want to destroy the very system they're now dependent upon to crossover. All you need to do is tell us how to reverse the curse, or who we need to speak to. If we must find a Romany, then so be it."

"You won't get a straight answer out of a gypsy," Theo said. "They lie as adeptly as they steal."

"You don't understand," Jacob said. "The curse has not been spoken only a single time, it has happened twice now, and the Administrators are none the wiser as to who did it."

"Twice? So there were two people involved? How remarkable to have two people prepared to die to achieve such an end. At least they're gone now. Oh Jacob, this means your murderer is dead!" I clasped his hand but he shook his head.

"You're right in that there may be more than one person involved, but not in the way you think. You see, both times the culprit has not stayed in the Waiting Area after he has delivered the curse. He, or she, returns here to the living realm."

"Here!" I shook my head. "That's not possible. Dead is dead."

"Unless he's brought back to life."

CHAPTER 4

Good lord! Brought back to life after intentionally dying? To put oneself through such an ordeal in order to deliver a curse was truly extraordinary, and incredibly dangerous. It was the act of a desperate individual.

"Emily?" George bobbed down to look me in the eyes. "Are you aware your mouth has flopped open?"

"What did he say?" Theo asked, resting a steady hand on my shoulder.

I repeated Jacob's words and was met with gasps of horror.

"But...why?" Theo asked. "Why go to such lengths?"

"Because he hates me," Jacob said. I did not repeat his words for Theo and George. We all knew the story of Jacob's murder, of how his killer blamed him for Frederick's death although we were not sure how that could be his fault.

"Because he has nothing to lose," I said, answering Theo.

Jacob's gaze held mine. "Or nothing to live for." He may have been faint, but I could see violent waves of emotion rippling through him. He knew he was the cause of the turmoil in the Waiting Area, albeit indirectly, and it troubled him deeply.

"If he must die to deliver the curse," Theo said, frowning,

"why can't anyone up there identify who it is?"

"A good point," I said. "Surely the Administrators have seen them come then go again."

Jacob shook his head. "There is a moment of uncertainty, where life hangs in the balance and death has not fully taken hold. It's very brief, but in that time, the spirit is in transit."

"In transit?"

"Traveling from this realm to the Waiting Area. It's like a long, dark tunnel with a light at the other end. No one in the Waiting Area can see into it, including the Administrators, yet the spirit cannot see out either."

"But they can speak?"

"Yes, if they have their wits about them. Most spirits are so shocked by their death and frightened about what will greet them at the end of the tunnel that speaking is the last thing on their mind. Whoever is saying the curse is aware of the transition process and aware of how long they have until they're completely dead and cannot return."

"Someone must be bringing him back to life," I whispered. "That's why you think more than one person is involved."

Jacob nodded and I repeated what he'd said for Theo and George's benefit.

"Amazing," George muttered. He pushed his glasses up his nose and squinted at the bookshelves. "Surely one of these has something useful."

"I doubt it," Theo said. "If this is a gypsy curse, then we'll need a gypsy to learn more about it. The ones I've met cannot read or write."

"Why hasn't the Waiting Area been completely destroyed?" I asked Jacob. "A minute is long enough to utter a curse so one trip should have sufficed, yet our villain has been twice and still the Waiting Area exists."

"Each utterance of the curse is only enough to do partial damage," Jacob said. "It doesn't seem strong enough to destroy it completely."

"Which begs the question, how many times does it need

to be spoken before the Waiting Area disappears entirely?"

"The Administrators don't know. It could be done on the next visit, or it could take a few more. Certainly not more than a handful."

We fell into a heavy silence until Theo broke it. "Let me walk you home, Emily. We don't want your sister to worry."

"Go," Jacob said. "He's right and there is nothing more we can do today."

I passed near him and brushed his fingers. His hand curled into a fist and he turned away, ignoring me. Ignoring the spark between us.

"If I learn anything else, I'll come to you immediately," he said.

If you can.

My stomach rolled and I felt a little faint myself. The thought of not seeing Jacob again for the rest of my life was awful enough, but knowing I would not see him again in the Otherworld after my death made my heart ache. We could *not* allow the destruction of the Waiting Area to continue.

Jacob blinked off and George walked Theo and me to the entrance hall. His mother breezed through as the footman opened the door. "You're still here?" she said, although whether she addressed me or Theo I couldn't tell.

"We were just leaving," I said, edging around her wide burgundy skirt.

She untied her hat and handed it to the footman hovering at her elbow. "You were quite the topic of discussion today among my friends, Miss Chambers."

"Oh?"

"Mother, you know that Emily is a medium," George said. "Do you need to bring up your views now?"

Mrs. Culvert didn't believe in the paranormal. Or rather, she didn't care for it. She may have been married to a demonologist and have a son who shared his interests, but she didn't like discussing anything of that nature. It was social suicide as far as she was concerned, and so she never chatted to me about ghosts. We all preferred it that way.

"Your recent entertainments have become quite the talk among ladies of consequence," she said, pouting sympathetically at me. "Or rather, the *lack* of entertainment."

"Mother," George ground out. "Don't."

"Such a shame. When I first told my friends that we'd become acquainted they were all aflutter, wanting me to host one of your displays."

"It's called a séance," George said.

I could feel Theo's hand at my back, the gentle pressure reassuring.

"I was never overly keen on the idea, myself," she went on. "I endured enough hocus pocus when Mr. Culvert was alive. Anyway, it seems it no longer matters because no one wants me to host a séance now. You see, Lady Willoughby was quite disappointed that you could not summon her father's ghost, and of course we all know how prone to gossip *her* friends can be. The whole of London has heard about your failure." She placed a gloved hand on my arm. "Do tell me when you're able to see spirits again. My friends will be most interested to be first in line and I'm prepared to accommodate them this one time, for your sake. No need to thank me." She trotted off toward the grand staircase, her heels click-clacking on the tiles.

"I'm sorry, Emily," George said. "Ignore her. She's not got the faintest idea what you do and how the spirit world works."

I sighed. "Not many do."

"Come, Emily." Theo crooked his elbow. "Take my arm and we'll talk of balls and gowns and happier things on the walk."

Theo did indeed talk of happier things, but I didn't listen very closely. My head was filled with miserable thoughts.

"I've been poor company, and I'm sorry," I said when he delivered me to my front door.

"No need to apologize." He pushed back a curl of my hair that had come loose in the Druids Way breeze. "I enjoy being near you even when you say nothing."

A little flare lit inside me, spreading its warmth. "You're very sweet."

"And you are very interesting." He dipped his head and lifted my chin with his finger. "I cannot stop staring at you," he murmured.

He was going to kiss me, right there on my doorstep. My body hummed with pleasure and my skin tightened at the prospect. Yet I did not reach up to him. It would be disloyal to Jacob. He was still a very big part of my life, even though he wanted me to be with Theo, and even though I knew Theo would be good for me.

But before I could step back, Theo closed the gap between us. His lips caressed mine, the kiss hesitant and uncertain. God help me, I did not pull away. I wanted it. Wanted to be adored and cherished, wanted to hear his compliments and *feel* how much he liked me.

He deepened the kiss and his hands caught me round the waist, gently pulling me closer, closer, until our bodies met. His tongue teased mine and one hand gently pressed into my back, holding me to him. My mind reeled with a riot of sensations and emotions that I couldn't separate or identify. I couldn't think. Didn't want to. Theo was here and alive and I *needed* him, needed this.

"Emily," he murmured against my lips. "Oh, Emily, I love you."

I broke the kiss and gasped.

"I...I'm sorry." He shuffled his feet and looked down at his shoes. "I spoke too freely, you're not ready. Forgive me?"

Air. I needed air. My chest rose and fell with the effort to breathe. "No. Yes, I forgive you. I mean no, there's nothing to forgive." I was such a bumbling idiot.

He chuckled. "I should not have declared myself yet, but...I couldn't help it. Having you here, in the semi-dark, kissing you...it's all quite exhilarating." He breathed deeply and let it out slowly. "I had better go before I turn into a blathering fool and tell you your eyes are prettier than the stars in the sky."

I laughed. "Oh dear, that is bad."

He chuckled. "Goodnight, Emily."

"Goodnight, Theo."

He didn't leave immediately, but kissed the back of my hand instead. His lips were as warm and soft as pillows. Then, wordlessly, he bowed and trotted down the stairs. I waved and turned to go inside.

The door opened and Celia's head popped round. "Did he kiss you?"

"Celia!"

"I couldn't see from the window. Well? Did he?"

"None of your business." I pushed past her into the hall. Both Lucy and Cara stood there, watching. Lucy's cheeks were a bright pink and her eyes twinkled. Cara looked grave. "Have you all been waiting here the whole time?"

"From the moment we spotted you both walking up to the house," Celia said as Lucy took my hat and coat. "Now, I don't mind him kissing you, Emily, but perhaps not on the front doorstep next time. You know how nosy the neighbors are, and they're terribly old fashioned about these sorts of things. Not like me."

I groaned. Celia would have me wed to Theo in a trice if it were in her power.

"He did kiss you, didn't he?"

"Celia!"

She sighed. "Emily, I'm not prying. Really." She waited until Lucy disappeared into the kitchen area at the back of the house then she took both my hands. "As your elder sister, I need to know what that young man's intentions are. Has he declared himself in any way?"

I withdrew my hands. "Not yet." I would not tell her he'd declared his love for me. The memory made me hot all over and a little light-headed. I didn't know what to think. It was too much to take in, and I wanted to keep it to myself a little longer. Something just for me.

"Very well." She pressed her fingers to her temple and rubbed. "We must focus now on the ball. If he has not given you an indication of his intentions by that night, you'll have to make yourself available to the other gentlemen in attendance. Do not dance more than once with Theo. We'll discuss it more as the evening approaches."

I turned to Cara and rolled my eyes. She pressed her lips together in an attempt not to smile.

"Don't you want to hear what we learned about the problem in the Waiting Area?" I asked them.

"Yes," Cara said, once more the grave little girl of our first encounter. A girl with too much responsibility for such small shoulders.

"Of course, tell us everything," said Celia. "I'm so distracted this evening. It must be because of your young man."

"Or because of the man who was here earlier," Cara said.

"Cara, hush."

"Who was here earlier?" I asked.

"My brother," Cara said. "Louis."

Celia clicked her tongue. "Never mind that now." She grabbed my hand and pulled me into the drawing room. "Lucy will have dinner ready soon and I don't want to alarm her with all this talk of spirits. Tell us what you learned from Mr. Culvert's books."

"Not until you've told me about Louis' visit. What did he say? Goodness, Celia, this is monumental! Were you even going to tell me?"

She opened her embroidery basket and removed her latest creation, a cushion cover in Christmas reds and greens. "Of course I was. When the time was right."

"That time would be now."

She sat on the sofa beside Cara and I sat in the armchair near the fireplace. A small fire burned in the grate, chasing the spring chill from the room.

"There is nothing to tell." She looked up. "That reminds me, you deliberately disobeyed me and went to see François Moreau at the market. Emily, I'm so disappointed in you. You constantly lie to me lately." She stabbed her needle through the cushion cover. "What has gotten into you? It's that Beaufort ghost, isn't it?" she said without pausing to let me answer. "Ever since he came into our lives, you've been getting into trouble."

"Don't blame Jacob. Circumstances beyond his control, beyond everyone's, have meant I need to do things I wouldn't usually do."

"I don't see how visiting François Moreau has anything to do with Beaufort or other supernatural events."

"Wait a moment." I leaned forward, but she did not look up from her stitching. "Did Louis tell you Cara and I went to the market?"

"No."

"I didn't say anything either," Cara chimed in.

"Then how did you know I'd been to see my grandfather?" I asked Celia.

She lifted one shoulder and concentrated on her embroidery.

"You went to see him too, didn't you? Celia, I don't know what's got into you of late," I mimicked.

She glanced up sharply. "This is not a joke, Emily."

I sank into the deeply cushioned back of the armchair. "Did you see Louis?" She nodded once and my heart lifted. "Are you going to tell me what he said?"

"There is nothing to tell. We talked very little. He told me he was back in England briefly and would soon return to the colonies. He cannot be away from his business for long. Apparently he has established a greengrocer shop in a place called Melbourne that is doing exceedingly brisk trade. He plans to diversify into other goods next year and perhaps open another shop."

"And what did he say when you told him about me?"

She pulled the needle through the fabric and I waited as she completed another stitch. I continued to wait and when she didn't answer, I heaved myself out of the chair. "You didn't tell him, did you? Celia!"

"It wasn't an appropriate time."

"Not appropriate!" My fists, heart, and very insides clenched.

"Calm down." She laid her embroidery in her lap. "We only spoke for a few minutes. I...I merely wanted to learn how long he was in London for and what the nature of his business is here. I left after I got answers."

"Why?" I threw my hands up. "Celia, why didn't you talk longer or invite him to dinner?"

"Seeing him again brings back too many painful memories." She sniffed and looked down at her embroidery but did not pick it up. "Please, Emily, I don't wish to speak of him anymore." She spoke so quietly I could barely hear her.

Cara and I looked at each other. She shrugged. I sighed. "I do want to see him before he leaves," I said.

"I know." Celia gave me a watery smile. "And you will. I'll make sure of it. Just...not yet. Let me get used to the idea of him being here again. I'll be more prepared next time. Seeing him today was quite a shock."

It must have been. My sister's feathers rarely looked so ruffled. "Very well," I said, unable to keep the frustration out of my voice entirely.

Celia took up her embroidery again and resumed stitching. "Tell us what you learned today."

I told them about the gypsy curse and how it was delivered to the Waiting Area. At the end, Cara sat perfectly still, her big brown eyes staring at me. She said nothing, but her fear was so palpable I could almost feel it.

"How diabolical!" Celia muttered, her embroidery once more forgotten.

"Indeed," I said. "To do something so dangerous and so drastic, Jacob's murderer must be very angry and be adamant that he was the cause of Frederick's demise."

"His parent," Celia said with absolute certainty. "Remember Jacob told you his murderer said 'my son.' That would explain the risk and the dogged determination to get revenge."

"We need to find Frederick Seymour's parents. Lady Preston's enquiries met a dead end there, pardon the pun. The Seymours no longer live at the address the university had listed for them and the new occupants didn't know where they'd gone. Finding them will be key to this, I know it."

Lucy entered and announced dinner was ready. Celia packed her embroidery away in the basket and headed out of the drawing room. I went to follow her, but Cara caught my sleeve.

"Will Mr. Beaufort be able to do something to stop the curse?" she asked.

"I don't know. We know so little about it."

"But will he...will he be all right?"

My throat tightened. I felt like the world was spinning out of control, or that I was the one spinning while the world remained unmoving around me. I grasped her hand and held on, anchoring myself. "I don't know."

"Will *you*?" she whispered. "Be all right, I mean?"

I bent and kissed her forehead. "Of course."

At the dinner table, conversation stalled. It seemed no one wished to discuss the curse or Louis, so I changed the topic entirely. "What time is the séance tomorrow?" I asked my sister.

"We don't have a séance tomorrow." She reached for the bowl of parsnips. "It's been canceled."

"Canceled?"

"As has our evening one, and the two for the day after."

I lowered my fork. "Oh no."

"All will be well," she said rather too chirpily to convince me. "Don't worry. We still have more set up for the rest of the week and into the next two."

I wish I could be so confident. I suspected this was only the beginning. First Lord Preston's threat then Mrs. Culvert's comment about my flagging reputation—I had a feeling it was only a matter of time before more séances were canceled.

I helped Lucy clear away the dishes because I didn't feel like reading a book and I wasn't fond of embroidery or sewing. Celia was helping Cara with her reading, and I needed company. I hated being alone of late. It gave me too much time to think and thinking led to an overwhelming sadness.

We took the plates and bowls into the small scullery off the kitchen and Lucy washed as I dried. It was nice that she didn't fear me anymore and she chatted incessantly about this and that in her bubbly manner.

"I saw a friend at Leather Lane market today when I went with Miss Chambers to see that mad grocer," she said. "It was so nice to see her. We used to go to the servants' school together and she said something to warm my heart. You'll never believe it, but she saw our lovely Mrs. White last week."

"Mrs. White!" I stopped drying. "What about her?"

"She's got herself a position as a governess at a fancy lord's house. Quite a step up from the school."

The "school" was the North London School for Domestic Service, a charity-funded organization in the poor parish of Clerkenwell. They taught orphans the skills needed to be servants and helped them find employment at the end of their term. It's how we'd found Lucy. It kept the most desperate children off the streets and out of the clutches of pickpocket and prostitution gangs.

Unfortunately the previous master of the school, Mr. Blunt, had helped release the shape-shifting demon and had generally been an unpleasant fellow. Jacob had scared him out of London but when the strange paranormal events continued, we'd gone looking for him. However, he'd disappeared entirely, as had Mrs. White, one of the teachers who was much loved by her pupils. We'd wanted to ask her if she knew where we could find Blunt, but I'd grown worried when I heard she'd claimed to be going to her sister's house. She didn't have a sister.

"Did your friend say which house she's working in?" I

asked.

"Somewhere in Grosvenor Street." Lucy swiped a pale wisp of hair off her forehead with the back of her hand. "Why do you want to know?"

"I, uh..."

"You can tell me, miss. I won't break a confidence."

"I'm not worried about that, Lucy, I trust you. It's just that I don't want to alarm you."

"Ah." She handed me a wet plate. "It's a spirit matter?"

"Yes." I eyed her closely. "Does that frightens you?"

She lifted one shoulder. "Not like it used to. That Mr. Beaufort's ghost, he's been nice and all. He don't throw things about like I thought he would."

"Only angry ghosts do that." And there were many of those. Spirits could cross from the Waiting Area into the Otherworld whenever they wanted, but some chose to stay and haunt the place of their death because they had something they wanted to resolve first. That's why I was frequently called to haunted homes—to rid it of an unhappy spirit who took their unhappiness out on their bereaved family. Or in some cases, the not so bereaved.

At least, that's how it used to work. With the curse causing chaos, it seemed no ghosts could cross, nor could they stay here.

"Does Mrs. White have a ghost problem?" Lucy asked.

"She might be able to help me with a supernatural situation," I said. "I won't know until I've spoken to her. Do you know which house on Grosvenor Street?"

"Sorry, miss, my friend didn't say."

"That's all right, I'll find her. Now, let's speak of happier things."

"Like the ball?"

I smiled. "Like the ball."

***

I awoke some time during the night with the peculiar sense of being watched. But I wasn't afraid.

"Jacob," I whispered into the darkness.

His shadowy figure emerged from the corner of my bedroom. "I'm sorry. I shouldn't be here," he said. "It's very bad manners."

"I'm not sure social conventions still apply after death."

"They should. I like to think they do in my case, although...around you...my thoughts are far from gentlemanly."

My heart skidded to a halt. I knew what he meant and it filled me with warm pleasure from head to toe.

I sat up and put out my hand. Ghosts could see better than when they were alive. I was acutely aware that I wore nothing but my nightgown and my hair must look a fright. "Why are you here?" I asked. "Is something wrong?"

He took my hand. He was so very cold and I felt him shiver. "I simply wanted to see you, Em. Do I need another reason?"

"You don't but...but lately you've been avoiding me."

"You know why." His voice was dark and thick, clogged with heavy emotion.

"Do I?"

"Theo is a good man," he said. "I like him more and more. I'm not going to get in the way."

It's what I wanted too of course. So why did I feel so empty all of a sudden? "He is a good man, as you say." He must have seen me kiss Theo, otherwise why bring it up at all? I wondered if he knew how much I'd enjoyed it, but how much I'd wished *Jacob* had been the one kissing me.

"You have a real chance of a happy life with him, Em. A full, long life."

"Don't," I choked out.

"No, listen to me." He caught my face in his hands but quickly let go and stepped away from the bed. "Don't throw this opportunity away. You like him. You enjoy his company, I know you do."

"That doesn't mean I want to marry him."

"Not yet perhaps, but one day." His voice drifted off to a tired whisper. "I must go. Sleep well."

He left and my bedroom seemed darker with the loss of him. I lay down and must have fallen asleep because the next thing I knew Cara was at my bedside, shaking me. "Emily, come quickly! Louis is here."

CHAPTER 5

"Louis!" I sat up with a start. "So early?"

"It's late," Cara said. "You overslept."

I glanced at the clock on the mantelpiece. It was ten o'clock. I sprang out of bed and threw off my nightgown.

"He arrived unannounced and won't leave." Cara's eyes shone and I suspected she was quite thrilled by this piece of news. "Celia is very cross. She keeps asking him to leave, but he refuses and says she has to hear him out first. Come quick, Emily, or you'll miss him."

Celia would be furious, but I didn't care. It was time I met my father. Time he was made aware of my existence. Celia would have to come to terms with it.

"Help me dress," I said.

Miraculously, I was ready in five minutes, although my hair was not. There was no time to arrange it. "Come, Cara," I said. "Hold my hand."

Despite the reassurance her presence gave me, I had to pause at the top of the stairs to catch my breath and settle my nerves. Cara squeezed my hand. In my fluster, I'd forgotten that Louis probably didn't know about her either, and she must be wondering what reaction he'd have when he found out. It would be an uncertain time for her too.

We held hands and entered the drawing room together. Celia sat on the sofa. A tall man stood near the fireplace, his back to us. He had short, black hair, and the skin on the back of his neck was browner than mine.

My father.

I gave an involuntary gasp and both Celia and Louis turned. My sister glared at me for a brief moment then her gaze faltered and she looked down at the clasped hands in her lap. Her knuckles were white. Louis simply stared. First at me, then at Cara, then back at me.

Celia sniffed but did not introduce us. It would seem she had thrown her manners out the door when he arrived.

Cara stepped forward and performed a small curtsey as Celia had taught her. "I am Miss Cara Moreau," she said in a bold voice. "Your sister."

"Sister!" His eyes widened. "I have a sister?"

"Half-sister."

"Ah. François' child." He bowed and when he straightened, there was a small smile on his lips. "Good morning, Miss Moreau. Or perhaps I should call you Cara since we are brother and sister. You didn't tell me you'd contacted my relations, Celia."

The informal use of her first name drew another little gasp from me. Celia did not look up.

"And you must be another sister," he said to me, bowing again. "I'm pleased to meet you. I wish my father had told me of your existence. I would have liked to know I had family."

"I am not your sister." My heart smashed against my ribs and my mouth suddenly went dry. I had imagined this moment many times, and in my imagination I had been confident, charming and certain of what I would say. Now I could barely find my voice. "My name is Emily Chambers. I'm your daughter."

He staggered. His jaw dropped open as if it were on a loose hinge. "My...daughter?" He looked me up and down, his mouth still open, his brow deeply furrowed. "Emily."

Slowly, slowly, his brow cleared, but his eyes clouded. "I have a daughter. A child," he murmured. Then he shook his head and smiled sheepishly. "Hardly a child. You must be seventeen?"

I nodded. I didn't trust my voice, not yet. My heart still beat furiously, but now that the first awkward moment was over, my nerves calmed a little. He hadn't walked out and hadn't denied that he was my father. And he'd smiled.

"My sister has been a great comfort to me since our mother died," Celia said. She took my hand and drew me down so hard onto the sofa, I thought my shoulder would wrench out of its socket. "I would have been all alone without her companionship."

His gaze settled on Celia and her grip tightened on my hand. There was something between them. Something unsettling. I had the very distinct feeling she didn't like him.

"Your mother?" He crossed his arms and narrowed his eyes. I thought he was going to ask us not to mention the woman he'd apparently loved enough to beget a child on, but he did not. He grunted as if he'd come to a decision, then said, "May I ask why you never told me about Emily?"

Celia stiffened. "If we'd known where to send letters, we would have. But you did not write to us when you arrived in New South Wales as promised."

Louis didn't deny it and my heart constricted. So it was true. Part of me had hoped there'd been a mistake, but it seemed Louis hadn't wanted to remain in touch once he arrived in the colony of New South Wales, despite the assurances he'd given Mama before he left.

"You didn't mention her yesterday," Louis said. "Or my sister. Does she live here? The old man is crazy. I don't want her near him."

"It's a little late to worry about your family," Celia snapped.

I squeezed her hand, but she snatched it away and smoothed down her skirts.

"I live here now," Cara said. "They've been very good to

me. I'm learning how to be a proper lady."

Louis smiled, but it wasn't gentle. There was something of a harsh sneer to it. "Celia would be good at that. She knows all about being a *proper* lady."

My sister stood abruptly. "I think you should leave."

"No!" I stood too, ready to run across the room and block Louis' exit if necessary. "Wait. I have so many questions." But where to start? I needed to say something before Celia marched him out. "Why didn't you write?"

Louis lifted his chin and his jaw went rigid. "I meant to. But circumstances...I got into some difficulty in New South Wales..." He regarded Celia from behind half-lowered lids. "I don't wish to discuss it. Some things are best left forgotten."

Celia made a miffed sound through her nose. "We agree on that, at least." She strode to the door. "If you don't mind, Mr. Moreau, we have a very busy day ahead of us."

"But I haven't finished with him yet," I said. "Mr. Moreau...Louis..."

"Father?" He laughed nervously.

"Father." A lump lodged in my throat. I'd never called anyone that. It was so hard to believe that I'd finally met him. And he was handsome and had kind eyes, like I'd imagined. They were brown and large like mine. I could see why Mama had fallen in love with him. Seventeen years ago he must have been very young indeed, but I suspect he'd been mature for his age. Someone with a father like François would have to grow up fast to take care of himself.

"Ask me anything," he said.

"No," Celia snapped. "Emily, have you forgotten what it is you need to do today?"

"No, but—"

"Perhaps another time, Emily," my father said gently. "When we've all had a chance to calm down and think about things." He looked to Celia who tilted her chin at him. "I'm not leaving London just yet."

"You said you were sailing within a few days!" Celia blurted out. "Well. Another broken promise."

He drew in a long breath and let it out slowly. "At least I haven't lied."

"You've refused to answer questions about your last seventeen years and refused to tell us why you did not write. An omission is as good as a lie."

"As I told you yesterday," Louis said through a clenched jaw, "the timing of my departure depends on one matter in particular and in which way it's resolved. I had hoped for a quick resolution, I admit, but I've discovered that it's not going to be quick at all. Now that I have learned about Emily, I will not be leaving in a hurry. My business is in my partner's hands and I trust him completely."

"You must be good friends," I said, more to ease the tension than anything else.

"We are." His voice softened. "I saved his life and he's been the best of friends to me ever since."

"You saved a man's life? How very noble of you."

He dismissed my gushing comment with a shake of his head. "Until next time, daughter." He bowed at me then at Cara then fronted up to Celia. My sister didn't meet his gaze. "I will return soon. It would be nice if we could be polite to each other, Celia, but I understand if you cannot. It's clear you can't bear the sight of me."

She stormed off but stopped at the doorway when she realized he wasn't following. "The front door is this way, Mr. Moreau."

He was leaving and I hadn't asked him all the things I'd wanted to. Why had he come back after all this time? Why hadn't he contacted Mama when he was settled in New South Wales? Why had he left in the first place? I knew he'd applied for the government assistance scheme to move to that far-off land and been accepted, but why apply at all? Was he that unhappy here in England?

"It's because of Mama, isn't it?" I said, the words tumbling out before I could stop them. "That's why you left."

"Pardon?" Celia said, straining toward us without moving

her feet. "What did you say, Emily?"

Louis stared at me.

"My mother didn't love you enough, did she? You must have seen how much she loved Papa—I mean, the man she married. He may have died, but she still loved him deeply. That's why you left. Because you knew she'd never love you enough. You had to get away in order to forget her."

He glanced at Celia. She looked startled at the attention at first, then her face hardened. "I don't know how much your mother loved me," he said softly. "She was very...closed on the matter of her heart."

"What are you saying?" Celia said, striding up to us. "Mr. Moreau, I've asked you to leave."

"Will you not call me Louis?"

"It wouldn't be proper."

He gave a grudging laugh. "Always fixated on propriety, aren't you?"

"Not always," Celia said levelly.

His nostrils flared. He said nothing for what seemed an eternity. My sister looked away first and he finally turned to me. "Emily, I would dearly like to get to know you better while I'm here. You too, Cara. I've never had a sister or daughter before."

"You don't have a family in New South Wales?" I asked.

"I live in Victoria now, a colony to the south of New South Wales. And no, I don't have a family anywhere. Except here, that is."

I waited for more. Indeed, we all three waited, but he didn't tell us why he'd spent seventeen years alone when he could have wed or fathered more children. Or come home to England. Louis bowed again and without another word, strode out of the drawing room. Neither Cara, Celia nor I followed him out, and I heard Lucy chatting to him in the hall before the front door opened and shut.

Celia was the first to speak. "Well." She sat down and picked up her embroidery basket. "At least that's done. Now we can all get on with our lives." She hummed a tune as she worked her needle, but her shaking hand gave away her true state of mind. She was as disturbed by Louis' visit as I was.

***

I wanted to tell Jacob about my father, but didn't want to summon him. Visiting our realm took energy and he needed to conserve it. His weakness worried me terribly.

Cara and I shared our thoughts out of Celia's hearing. She seemed just as excited to have a brother as I was to have a father. I also spoke to George about Louis when I went to his house.

"I'm very pleased for you," he said as we waited in the hall for his carriage to be brought around from the stables. "Very pleased. So you're not an orphan after all."

"I suppose I'm not."

The carriage arrived and George gave his driver instructions to drive to the house of Lord and Lady Preston. We wanted Mr. Seymour's address from Lady Preston. We knew he had moved, but perhaps the new residents could give us a clue as to where he'd gone, or of how to find the elusive Mrs. Seymour. Lady Preston had already spoken to them, but it was worth trying again.

"I would not hold out much hope if I were you," Lady Preston said to us as we stood in her private parlor. Weak morning light struggled through the large windows, casting an insipid glow over the spindly Georgian furniture. She rifled through her desk drawer and produced a folded piece of paper. "Here it is."

I took it because George was too preoccupied to notice. He was looking over his shoulder at the door, probably hoping Adelaide would enter. I hoped Lord Preston would not.

"What will you do if you cannot find the Seymours?" Lady Preston asked.

"I have another line of enquiry to follow," I said.

She gave a firm nod. "Good. I hope you are able to find something, Miss Chambers." She rested a delicate hand on my arm but there was strength in her grip. "If there is anything I can do, anything at all, please ask. If you require assistance or money, I will give it to you." Her intense blue stare, so like Jacob's compelled me to nod. "Do not be afraid of my husband. You are welcome here, despite his blustering. He is..." She swallowed. "He is still very affected by Jacob's death. It's not an excuse for his abominable behavior toward you, but..." Tears welled in her eyes and she looked away.

I laid my hand over hers. "I understand. I hope one day he will realize we're trying to help his son, but you need to prepare for the fact he never will. The existence of spirits is not something everyone can accept. I suspect Lord Preston is one of those."

"It doesn't matter what he believes, it only matters that Jacob is allowed to finish the journey he's already begun. I want him to crossover and find peace."

I did not tell her about the curse on the Waiting Area and how it was affecting all the spirits, including Jacob. There was nothing she could do and she didn't need the extra worry.

"Oh, Emily," said Adelaide, breezing into the parlor. "What a pleasant surprise. And Mr. Culvert too." She smiled at me, but she positively beamed at George. He blushed a fierce red.

"The pleasure is all ours, Miss Beaufort," George said. "I mean mine. The pleasure is mine. Unless it's Emily's too, but I can't speak for her."

Adelaide held out her hand and George took it and bestowed a kiss on the back. His face remained the color of radishes, but he didn't attempt to hide it.

"Did you receive my last letter, Miss Beaufort?" he asked. "I copied out those pages you asked for."

Adelaide bit her lower lip and glanced at her mother. "Yes, thank you. It was an interesting treatise."

"You've been writing to each other?" Lady Preston's smile stretched thin. "Adelaide, why didn't you tell me?"

"I...uh...I've recently discovered I have an interest in the supernatural. I didn't think you'd approve of my visiting Mr. Culvert to look at his library, so I wrote to him instead with my questions. He has been very good in responding with perfectly copied tracts from his books as well as his own thoughts. We've had some lively debates."

"You're right, I would not have approved. Nor would your father. Not in light of...recent plans."

Adelaide's nose wrinkled. "You mean my pending engagement to the Duke of Sandridge's son?"

"Bertie?" George cried. He must have realized how loud he'd said it because he muttered an apology. "Congratulations, Miss Beaufort." Poor George, I'd never seen him look so miserable. His face sagged as much as his shoulders.

"It's not settled yet."

"It soon will be." Lady Preston's frosty glare met her daughter's. It was the sort of look that silently demanded the recipient keep quiet. I'd been the object of many such glares from Celia, but they rarely had the desired effect. I seem unable to do as I'm told.

"Does that mean you'll be a duchess?" I asked eagerly. Imagine that—me friends with the future Duchess of Sandridge!

George narrowed his eyes at me and I wished I could take it back. Of course being a duchess would not compensate for marrying someone you did not love. I was glad I wasn't in Adelaide's position. Children of nobility couldn't wed whomever they chose. They had to marry other nobility, and failing that, wealth. I, on the other hand, could wed the man I loved.

Unless he was dead, of course.

"Yes, but a betrothal between us is yet to be finalized." Adelaide turned so that she was no longer facing her mother. It was a direct slight and I felt uncomfortable. I had never seen Adelaide and her mother quarrel before. "Until then, there is still a chance of escape."

"Adelaide," her mother scolded.

"Father and the Duke of Sandridge have not decided upon my worth," Adelaide went on. "I believe His Grace the duke is holding out for another piece of Father's property to be added to my dowry. It's a lucrative tract of land and of course Father doesn't want to give it up without a fight. Not even for the prospect of being attached to a dukedom."

"That's enough," Lady Preston snapped.

"Unfortunately, poor, dear Bertie is rather sickly and there's always the chance he'll die before his father, in which case I'll never be a duchess. What a shame that would be, wouldn't it, Mother?"

Lady Preston had gone quite rigid. I expected her to berate her daughter, but she didn't. Indeed her lips were clamped together tightly, emphasizing the tiny lines around her mouth.

I took George's arm and steered him toward the door. "Thank you for the address, Lady Preston." I tugged George. He didn't seem to have his wits with him, but he followed me meekly enough, although he continued to look back at Adelaide.

We got as far as the exit. The dominating figure of Lord Preston blocked the doorway. My entire body groaned at the sight of him.

"What's she doing here?" he bellowed over my head.

Lady Preston sailed up to us. Her anger seemed to have dissolved and she was all solicitude as she smiled at her husband. "She came for—"

"I told you never to let her in. Did I not make myself clear? She is a disruptive influence on you and Adelaide."

"She is not," Adelaide protested.

There was a shocked silence, not only from her parents, but from George and I as well. I'd never heard her speak so disrespectfully to them. Indeed, she'd always seemed a little afraid of her father. The pending nuptials must have triggered the dormant rebel within.

"Emily is kind and has our best interests at heart," she added.

"Quiet, girl, you don't know what you're talking about."

I felt George tense, but he said nothing. I would have tried to leave, but Lord Preston and his wife were in the way. *Oh please, please, move.* I didn't want a confrontation. And what if Jacob popped in? He didn't need anything else to worry about.

"No, Father," Adelaide said, "*you* don't know what you're talking about because you refuse to believe what is as plain as that ugly nose on your face."

Lord Preston bared his teeth like an animal. "Go. To. Your. Room."

"Gladly." She lifted her chin and walked up to us. "See you at the ball," she said and kissed me on the cheek. "It promises to be quite a lively event."

That was an understatement.

"There will be no ball if you continue to behave in such a manner," her father said as he stepped aside to let her pass.

Lady Preston gasped. "But the invitations have already gone out."

Nobody said anything to that. I suspect it was too late to retract the invitations. Canceling the ball would give the gossips the impression all was not well in the Beaufort household, and that certainly wouldn't do.

I strode past Lord and Lady Preston and thought I'd gotten away safely, but Lord Preston's booming voice stopped me. George stopped too and remained close, bless him.

"I will be watching you at the ball, Miss Chambers," Lord Preston said. "If you so much as whisper about spirits or nonsense of that nature, you will be evicted. Understand?"

"I say!" George said.

"Reginald, please. She is our guest."

Lord Preston puffed out his thick chest. "That doesn't give her the right to come here and use her devious practices on you."

"She is not a fraud," George said. "I can vouch for—"

"Be quiet. The only reason I tolerate you is because

you're of gentle stock and haven't tried to take money in exchange for whatever it is you do. But be aware that I know all about that so-called Society to which you belong, and I will shut it down if a single member so much as utters anything of a paranormal nature in my hearing. Understand?"

"Perfectly." George didn't move and for a horrifying moment I thought he might march up to Lord Preston and punch him. The earl was built as solidly as a house. A physical confrontation would not end well for George.

I dragged him with me onto the landing and down the stairs. The footman saw us out and into the waiting carriage. It took me a moment to catch my breath and regain my wits, by which time we were already moving.

George sat opposite me, visibly seething. "That man! Abominable! To speak in such a rude manner to his own wife and daughter!"

And to you and me, I almost added. But I did not want to add fuel to his ire. He was fiery enough. "Have you and Adelaide really been writing to each other in secret?" I asked.

He blinked and his temper seemed to dampen. "I wasn't aware it was in secret until today." He sighed. "I'm afraid I got her into trouble. Do you think she'll forgive me?"

"I have no doubt she will."

"But what of her parents? I didn't think Lord Preston would like my writing to his daughter, but I had hoped Lady Preston wouldn't mind. I didn't know Miss Beaufort was set to wed Bertie." He pulled a face. "Nothing against the fellow, but he's not an ideal match for her. Not a winter goes by that he doesn't take to his bed for weeks. To think of such a vibrant, lovely creature as Miss Beaufort being shackled to a weak character." He shook his head sadly. "It's more than a shame. It's..." He shrugged, as if there were no words to explain how terrible such a future would be.

"I'm surprised her mother wishes her to marry him at all, if that's the case."

"Lord Preston is the head of that household, in every

sense of the word. I suspect he has given them no say in the matter and his wife must accept the marriage as much as their daughter."

"He does seem like the sort to disregard everyone's opinions except his own."

"Poor Miss Beaufort." He sighed. "She didn't deserve such treatment when she only spoke the truth."

"True. His nose *is* rather ugly."

That coaxed a laugh from him.

***

We traveled to Camden Town and the address Lady Preston had given me. It was a modest house, rather like my own, in a middle-class suburb and the occupants were polite but unhelpful. They didn't know where the Seymours had moved to. They had not dealt with them so could not even give me a description or a first name. It was as we suspected, but it was frustrating nevertheless.

"Now what?" George asked when we were back inside the carriage.

"Now we visit Mrs. White."

"You've found her?"

"My maid said she's governess to a family on Grosvenor Street."

"You think she'll be able to help us find Blunt?"

"We can only try."

"We don't even know if Blunt had anything to do with Mortlock's possession, or this latest curse. We can only link him to the shape-shifting demon. Are we drawing too long a bow, Emily?"

I shrugged. "I don't know, but I have no other ideas."

"Nor me. Very well, let's try her. Which house on Grosvenor Street?"

"I don't know."

"Jacob could find out. He could look into each one and report back when he's found her."

"I don't want to summon him. I'm afraid he's too weak in his current state and being here may weaken him further."

"Who are you calling weak?"

"Jacob!" I clasped his hand without thinking. He felt cool and damp, like a mist, yet still solid. He did not look solid, however. He flickered alarmingly. "He's here," I said rather stupidly. Of course George must know.

"I'll search the houses for her," Jacob said.

"No, you shouldn't."

"Are you sure you're up to this?" George asked, ignoring my frown.

"Tell Culvert not to worry about me. You too, Em. I want to help where I can. I *need* to help. Time is running out, as you can see."

I tried to hold back the tears suddenly pooling. Crying would achieve nothing. "Very well. Let's go and find Mrs. White."

CHAPTER 6

George and I waited in the coach as Jacob searched the houses of Grosvenor Street. Mayfair was an exclusive area, although not quite as fashionable as it used to be at the beginning of the century. Where most of the younger generation had moved to new homes in Belgravia, the older, more aristocratic set had remained in their imperial mansions where they could reign supreme over leafy Grosvenor Square and surrounds.

It did not take Jacob long before he reappeared beside me in the carriage. He shimmered for a few moments before finally staying put. He looked worn out.

"Are you all right?" I asked.

He pressed his thumb and finger into his eyes and nodded. "I found her."

I repeated this for George's benefit. "Which house?" he asked.

"Number twelve," Jacob said. "She's in the schoolroom with two girls of about Cara's age."

I repeated this to George. "Let's go." I climbed out of the coach before George, which he didn't like. It went against his gentlemanly nature—he couldn't hold my hand and help me down the steps if he was behind me.

"I'll search Mrs. White's room," Jacob said when we reached the door of number twelve.

"Do it discreetly," I said.

"Have you never known me not to be discreet?"

"Frequently."

He gave a feeble chuckle and blinked off.

"I'm worried about him," I said to George as we waited for our knock to be answered. "He is not very strong. Not like he used to be."

George tucked my arm into his. "We'll resolve this soon. Don't worry. I have an inkling that we're right and Blunt is involved somehow. I'm certain Mrs. White will know where to find him."

I didn't have nearly as much confidence, but I set my doubts aside when the butler opened the door. We asked to see the governess, and after his initial blink of surprise, he took us down to the service area in the basement and showed us to a parlor little bigger than a cupboard. Being a governess, Mrs. White was not treated like a family member, but nor was she as low as the servants. Considering George's status, I'd suggested we inquire at the front door, but it seemed not even gentlemen were allowed to speak to the governess in the formal drawing room. It was the basement for us.

In a way, meeting her in the servants' parlor was better, more intimate. We didn't have to wait long before she entered. She paused in the doorway and shock flickered through her gaze before she turned a sweet smile on us. "Miss Chambers, isn't it? And Mr. Culvert? This *is* unexpected. To what do I owe the honor of your company?"

"We're sorry to disturb you here at your new place of work, Mrs. White," George said, rising so she could take his seat. There were only two. "But we've had the devil of a time trying to find you, and we're very glad we finally did."

"You've been looking for me?" She bustled into the parlor, business-like. She was a plump, short woman, yet she moved with purpose and efficiency. She sat and George stood at my side. "Does it have something to do with that awful night? I recall it very vividly."

"Not quite," I said. I recalled that night too. We'd killed one villain, sent the demon back to the Otherworld, and banished Blunt from London. Jacob had haunted him until he was out of his wits with fear. No one at the school was sorry he'd departed in the middle of the night without a farewell, particularly the girls he used to visit in the dormitory when he thought everyone asleep.

"We returned to the school recently with the hope of speaking to you," I said. "Unfortunately you'd already left."

"I needed a change of scene." Mrs. White's fingers twisted in her lap, as if she were constantly tying and untying them. "It was a sudden decision."

"You didn't think to give anyone a forwarding address?" George asked, a little too bluntly in my opinion.

Mrs. White lifted her head. Her eyes shone with unshed tears. "I wanted to distance myself from that place. The memories of that night..." She shook her head and did not go on.

George fished out a handkerchief from his jacket pocket and handed it to her. She thanked him and dabbed at her eyes.

"You were very brave, Mrs. White," he said gently, his earlier curtness gone. "Very brave indeed. Not everyone who is confronted with the worst of the supernatural cope as well as you did that night."

I wasn't so convinced she was entirely telling the truth, not after the lie I knew she'd already told. "How is your sister, Mrs. White? That is where you went immediately upon leaving the school, isn't it?"

She sniffed and pressed George's handkerchief to her nose. "I don't have a sister," she said. "That's what I told the servants, so they wouldn't worry about me. A single woman with no family to care for her is a somewhat pathetic figure and I didn't want anyone's pity."

I could not fault her on that. I felt terrible for doubting

her honesty. "Yes, of course," I muttered and gave her a sympathetic smile. "I'm so glad you're set up nicely here. This is a lovely house. Are the family kind?"

"Very. Thank you for your concern, Miss Chambers. Now, you said you needed to ask me something. Please don't think I'm rushing your visit, but I do need to return to the girls. They're quite the little troublemakers when they're left alone too long."

"Of course," George said. "We hoped you could tell us where to find Mr. Blunt."

"Blunt? But I thought you were pleased to be rid of him. Indeed, we all were." She closed her eyes and shuddered. Her reaction made me wonder if she'd had unwelcome visits from him in the night too.

"Oh, we were," I said. "The man was horrible in every sense of the word."

"Which is actually why we need to find him," George said. At Mrs. White's frown, he added, "Something else is happening and we wonder if he might be involved."

"What do you mean 'something else'?" When George didn't answer, she said, "You can tell me. I know what happened that night at the school, remember. You can trust me not to succumb to hysterics."

"We know you wouldn't," I said. Yet I didn't want to tell her everything. She had not proved to me that she was entirely comfortable discussing the supernatural. So I gave her the shortened version. "There is a problem in the Otherworld that is stopping ghosts from crossing over. Does that make sense to you?"

"In a way." Her frown deepened. "You think Mr. Blunt is doing something to cause this problem?"

"It's merely a thought since he was involved in the demon's release. We think the two events may be connected."

"Of course. As a matter of fact, I do know where he is now."

"Excellent."

"He's gone to another school here in London."

"London! But we told him to leave the city altogether."

"He did," she said. "Very briefly. He found me upon his return only a week ago. He wanted an account of that last night at the school. I think he thought he was a little mad, and needed to be reassured of what he'd seen."

"What did you tell him?"

She shrugged. "I told him I saw flying objects too. I mentioned the ghost and your involvement as a medium...all of it. He seemed a little afraid at first, but then I think he was happy to hear a witness account that matched his own."

"He probably decided that seeing ghosts was preferable to being mad," I said.

"So where is he now?" George asked.

"He's been appointed head master of the Royal Masonic Institution for Boys. It's a charity school funded by the Freemasons to educate the sons of their poorer members."

Sons only. Thank goodness. Blunt couldn't be trusted around girls.

"It's located in Wood Green on Lordship Lane." Her hand-twisting became more rapid. "Please don't mention that I told you where to find him."

"Of course," George said, soothing. "We wouldn't think of putting you in such an awkward position."

Her smile was one of relief.

"Thank you," I said. "You've been very helpful and it was good to see you. Lucy sends her regards. She was quite pleased to discover your whereabouts."

"Lucy? Oh, your maid. Yes, of course. How is she?"

"As cheerful as ever. She has even come to accept my work, in her own way."

"I'm pleased to hear it. She was a good girl."

We thanked her and left the house through the servants' entrance. "Success!" George said as we strolled to the carriage.

I looked back to the house and bit my lip. Something was troubling me, but I couldn't put my finger on what. Mrs.

White had seemed perfectly lovely and had explained her lie about going to her sister. Perhaps it was her twisting fingers, or perhaps it was the fact that she'd not asked me how Lucy fared first.

I shook off my doubts. We'd got what we came for—an address for Blunt.

George gave the driver instructions to drive to the northern suburb of Wood Green then settled himself on the seat opposite me. "I wonder how Beaufort fared."

I looked out the window at number twelve again. The governess's room would be on one of the upper floors where the nursery, schoolroom, and children's rooms were located. There was no sign of him.

The coach rolled off. I was just about to ask George for his opinion on how best to confront Blunt when Jacob appeared. Indeed, 'appeared' may be too strong a word. He faded in and out and then disappeared altogether again.

"Jacob!" I called. "Jacob, are you there?" *Oh God, no. Please come back to me.* I pulled the window down and stuck my head out in the hope he'd navigated to somewhere nearby, but he was nowhere to be seen.

"Perhaps you shouldn't summon him," George said gently. "He may need to conserve energy."

I stared out the window and concentrated on stilling my rapidly beating heart. It didn't work.

Just as the carriage turned a corner, Jacob materialized beside me, albeit weakly. "You're here!" I said and threw my arms around him. It was like embracing a fog—his skin felt moist and no longer solid. My arms didn't go all the way through him like they would if I wasn't a medium, but he didn't feel altogether *there.*

"What's happening?" I asked, pulling away. I cupped his cheek and he turned to kiss my palm. "Jacob, answer me!"

He shook his head. "Can't." His voice was a rasping whisper. "Can't...stay." He disappeared completely, only to come back and utter, "Seymour." And then he was gone.

"Jacob! Jacob!" I turned to George and he caught both

my trembling hands in his. "What if he doesn't come back? What if he...?" I swallowed the lump in my throat. "What if he's...?"

"Don't think that way, Em. He'll be fine. He's strong, remember? Perhaps he only needs to rest awhile."

I bit back tears. "We have to stop them. Whoever is doing this...they must be stopped."

He nodded. "Perhaps Blunt will provide an answer."

I doubted Blunt would simply 'provide' us with anything. We might need to use force and I wasn't sure George was the right man for the job.

"Do you think we could collect Theo?"

"Of course." He pulled the window down, held onto his hat, and called out new directions to the driver. "Let's hope Hyde is at home," he said, pulling the window up again.

"Jacob said 'Seymour' just now. Do you think he found a connection to Frederick Seymour in Mrs. White's room?"

"An interesting thought."

"But what possible connection could there be? She has no family. Perhaps he traveled elsewhere during his absence and found something." Whatever it was would have to wait until Jacob could visit us again.

If he were able.

"Don't worry, Emily," George said. "He'll return soon. The man can't leave you alone."

I appreciated his attempt to bolster my mood and said so. "You're a good friend, George. The best."

"As are you. You'd be an even better friend if you could say some nice things about me to Miss Beaufort." He looked out the window and waved his hand in dismissal. "Only if the right moment arises, that is. Don't trouble yourself otherwise."

"It would be no trouble, but I have a feeling she already knows what you're like anyway." I suddenly wanted to embrace him. Since that would be awkward beyond endurance, I simply sat in silence as we made our way to the Arbuthnots' house in Kensington.

***

Mr. Blunt kept us waiting in the visitors' drawing room of the Royal Masonic Institution for Boys for much longer than politeness allowed. We'd given the servant Theo's name rather than mine or George's so that he wouldn't have us thrown out, yet after twenty minutes, I was beginning to think Blunt wasn't going to appear at all.

"Perhaps he saw our approach through a window and has decided to avoid us," George said.

"Then why not send the footman in to tell us he's not here?" I asked.

"Perhaps he's in the middle of teaching a class," Theo said.

We agreed to wait a little longer. Another ten minutes passed. George spent the time pacing the room, his hands behind his back and looking every bit the impatient gentleman. It was lucky the drawing room was generously proportioned so he could stretch his lanky legs properly. It wasn't at all like the Clerkenwell school where Blunt had previously worked. The furniture was much more solid and modern although there was little of it. Just a sofa, four chairs, a small desk and three round occasional tables. A lovely Oriental rug covered most of the floor, its red tones providing the otherwise masculine room with some feminine color. The enormous white marble fireplace took up a great deal of wall space and would throw out a lot of heat if it were lit.

"Are you all right, Emily?" Theo asked quietly. "I know there's much on your mind lately but you seem particularly distracted today."

"I'm sorry. I'm worried about this situation in the Waiting Area. If the culprit continues his campaign, all those spirits will be obliterated. It not only affects current spirits but future ones too."

"It is bad," he said gloomily.

Bad didn't even begin to explain the enormity of our problem. "I've always known there was somewhere to go after I die. Now if Jacob's killer is allowed to succeed there will be nothing."

"The ultimate death," he muttered, nodding.

"Precisely. The fate which awaits us is very final indeed."

"It's not a certainty, Emily. Don't give up." He took my hand and his big, strong fingers were a comfort. Two weeks ago when we'd first met, his hands had been covered with calluses from his work on his family's Shropshire farm, but now they were covered in ink stains.

When we'd collected him from his aunt's house, I'd been surprised that he was home. I'd expected to be told he was attending lectures, but he'd bounded down the stairs to join us and hustled us back into George's waiting carriage. When I questioned him about his presence, he said the lecturer was ill and lessons had been canceled for the day.

"There's something more though, isn't there?" He massaged my hand, his thumb tracing circles around each of my knuckles. "I mean, I know you're worried about the future for all ghosts, but...there's one in particular, isn't there? One whom you care about above all others."

"I...I don't know what you mean."

His gentle gray gaze met mine. I looked away. "Yes, you do. It's all right, Emily. I'd rather know than not. You cannot help your feelings for him. By all accounts, he's an enigmatic fellow. At least, he was in life. Only you can know what he's like in death."

I sat there feeling stupid, my tongue thick in my mouth. I didn't know what to say. He was right, of course. I had very strong feelings for Jacob. Yet I liked Theo too and didn't want him thinking I was leading him astray when my heart was engaged elsewhere.

"Jacob is dead, Theo," I said levelly. "We have no future together." It was something Celia reminded me about almost every day in one way or another. She would be proud to hear me say it aloud, particularly to Theo. Yet I felt sick to my stomach.

"Not until you—" He cleared his throat. "You know

what I mean."

Not until you die. It was a thought forever at the back of my mind, and not one I was willing to bring closer to the front. Yet it was always present, dogging every one of my actions and dreams. It was hard to plan for the future without wondering when it would come to an end so I could join Jacob.

Ice-cold fingers dug through my skin to my bones. For the first time since I'd considered the dark thought of joining Jacob, I wondered what I'd do if the curse succeeded and he became nothing. Would I want to wait a lifetime knowing I wouldn't meet him again in the Otherworld? Or would I rather be with him sooner and become nothing together?

"Besides, I have many more things on my plate than the Waiting Area problem." I tried to sound sunny when all I felt was immeasurable gloom through to my core.

"Oh? Like your father's return? That is definitely something cheerful."

"And there's Adelaide's ball," I added.

"Oh yes!" said George from the other side of the room. I hadn't realized he'd been listening. Perhaps he only had heightened hearing when Adelaide's name received a mention. "I, for one, cannot wait. You'll be there, won't you, Hyde?"

Theo nodded. "My cousin Wallace and I are both invited. Since he proclaims not to enjoy dancing, I suspect he'll spend most of the evening standing at the refreshments table."

"And gossiping," George said. "By all accounts, he knows everyone."

Everyone, including Frederick Seymour and Jacob Beaufort when they were alive. The reminder put a dampener on our cheery banter and plunged us once more into melancholy.

Thankfully we were quickly distracted by the door opening and the appearance of Blunt.

"Bloody hell!" he cried when he saw me. He spun on his

heel and would have walked right out again if he hadn't lost his balance. George caught him and staggered under the weight of the bigger man, almost dropping him.

"Steady on," George said, helping the headmaster to stand.

Blunt pressed the heel of his hand to his forehead and leaned heavily on George's arm. "How did you find out I was here?" he asked, his voice unnaturally thin.

"The spirit world can see a great many things," I said.

"Go away." The half of his face not covered by his extraordinarily bushy beard and moustache was pale, the skin glistening as if he were in the grip of a fever.

"Are you ill, Mr. Blunt?" I indicated George should help him to one of the chairs. "You look very unwell."

"Just go." He groaned and lowered his head into his hands. "I've done nothing wrong since...since then and I want no trouble."

"That's not why we're here, Mr. Blunt."

Theo and George took up positions on either side of him as he sat, but I doubted they would be needed in any strong-arm capacity. Blunt looked far too ill to run or be any physical threat to me. Indeed, I was quite sure I could land a harder punch than him at that moment. From the way he slumped in the chair, he looked like a shadow of the man we'd first met mere weeks ago.

"Bloody hell," he muttered. "Get on with it then."

"You might be ill, but there's no cause for bad language around ladies," George said.

"She's no lady. Go on, state your business, or I'll call the footmen." Blunt's unfocused gaze met mine and I was startled by the web of red lines crisscrossing the whites of his eyes.

George bent down to Blunt's level. "Call the footmen and Miss Chambers will unleash a spirit on you."

Blunt's gaze flicked from George to me to Theo. He did not look afraid, and for a man who'd shown considerable terror whenever Jacob visited him in the past, it was rather telling—he *must* have known I couldn't summon any spirits from the Waiting Area.

"Where did you go after leaving the Clerkenwell school?" I asked. "It could not have been here. The footman said you were appointed only a few days ago."

"I was in the country. Visiting family. I returned to London last week and applied for the position here when I heard it was vacant. As soon as it was granted, I moved in. It's a live-in position and I have rooms on the top floor. Satisfied, Miss Chambers?"

He got up to leave, but Theo put a hand to his chest and Blunt fell back into the chair again, as limp as a doll.

"Call off your thugs," he said to me. "I have to go. I have a, uh, very important appointment to keep. Very important."

"Not yet," I said.

A shudder wracked Blunt and any remaining color in his face drained until he was completely white. "I don't feel well. Please...let me go...I *need* to keep my appointment. I'm begging you."

"Do you know a youth named Frederick Seymour?"

He swallowed heavily and ground his fingers into his eye sockets. "Should I?"

"Do you know anyone by the name of Seymour?"

Another shake of his head which produced a loud groan. He clutched his hair, almost dragging it out by the roots. "Miss Chambers..." He began to rise but once again, Theo shoved him back.

"Do you know any gypsies?"

He pulled a face, although I couldn't be sure if it was because the thought of meeting a gypsy filled him with horror or he was going to throw up.

George looked at me and shook his head. I sighed. He was right, we weren't going to get anywhere by questioning Blunt. If he knew anything about the curse, he wouldn't freely admit it to us.

"Thank you for your time, Mr. Blunt, although—"

Blunt made a great heaving sound and propelled himself

out of the chair so fast that he tripped over the rug and landed on his hands and knees by the fireplace. A horribly demonic sound burst from the depths of him before he emptied the contents of his stomach in the grate. The contents of his pockets had emptied all over the rug near his knees.

George buried his nose and mouth in the crook of his arm.

"I think we should go," I said.

George and I walked quickly to the door. Instead of joining us, Theo bent beside the miserable figure of Blunt. He picked something up and pocketed it. The three of us left the Institution in a hurry.

"He knows something," I said once we were inside the carriage. "Did you see how he wasn't afraid when you threatened him with spiritual violence, George? He knows the ghosts cannot easily come here and we're rather powerless in that regard."

"That doesn't mean he's connected to whomever is responsible for the curse," George said. "He may have heard the rumors of your recent difficulty summoning spirits."

"Not Blunt, surely. He's the master of a charity school. It's unlikely those rumors have reached him yet." It was something Celia and I were counting on. We had as much business from ordinary folk as we did from the upper regions of society. Indeed, it was the middle classes who tended to take us more seriously, whereas we were mostly seen as frivolous entertainment by the wealthy and privileged. Lady Preston had begun to change that through her circle of friends, but all her good work was unraveling a little more each day.

George and Theo exchanged glances.

"Are you two hiding something from me?" I asked.

"Emily," said Theo gently, "you must prepare for the worst."

"The worst?"

"Your business may fail completely," George said.

"What?"

"Mother has reported that even more people are talking about you in a, er, somewhat negative light."

"My aunt said the same thing." Theo grimaced. "I'm sorry, Emily, but I think you'll find you have many more cancelations before the week is out."

Bloody hell. "Celia will go into a panic if that happens."

"And you?" Theo asked. "It is your livelihood too, after all."

"We'll survive. We must have built up some savings by now." I heaved a sigh. "By the time it runs out, we should both have found employment elsewhere. Perhaps Mrs. White can tell me how to become a governess." The prospect of leaving behind my work as a medium lifted my spirits a little. I was tired of being seen as an oddity. All my life, I'd been treated differently, partly because of my heritage, but mostly because it was known I could communicate with the dead. It made making new friends difficult. Those who believed me were generally afraid of me, and everyone else just assumed I was mad or a fraud.

"Good," George said. "I'm glad you'll be all right. Aren't you, Hyde?"

"Of course, of course."

"I do hope Blunt's illness isn't contagious," said George after a moment of silence.

"I don't think it is." Theo pulled a small package out of his pocket and unwrapped the brown paper to reveal a little pile of black powder.

"What is it?" I asked.

"I think I know," George said, adjusting his glasses and taking a closer look.

"So do I," Theo said.

"What is it?" I asked them. Neither answered. George sat back and Theo shuffled his feet. "Tell me!"

"It's opium," George finally said.

Theo nodded. "It seems Blunt is addicted to the stuff."

CHAPTER 7

"Opium! Good lord," I said. "I don't know much about it, but I do know having an addiction to it can be debilitating."

Theo folded the brown paper over the powder and tucked the parcel into his waistcoat pocket. "That explains why Blunt was sick. He must be due his next dose." He patted his pocket. *We* now had his next dose.

"That's what he must have meant about his appointment," I said. "Will he be all right? What will happen if he doesn't take it?"

Theo shrugged. "Culvert, do you know?"

George's nod was grim. "I do unfortunately. There was a fellow in the Society who was addicted to the stuff. He started smoking it to lessen the pain of a back injury obtained from a riding accident. After a few months, it no longer had the same effect and he needed to smoke more of the stuff to get some relief. That's when his health began to decline. He lost weight, lost his ability to focus, and looked ill all of the time. He ceased caring about everything and everybody, which I think was part of its allure. When he tried to give up, or when he hadn't smoked it for a period of time, he was very much like Blunt was now. Sick, shaking, terrible nightmares, and that was only on the nights he *could* sleep.

More often, he could not."

"I almost feel sorry for Blunt," I said.

"Was he like this the last time you met him?" Theo asked.

"No." I pressed a hand to my stomach, suddenly feeling a little ill myself. "Oh George, what have we done? What if Jacob's haunting was the reason Blunt took up the habit in the first place?"

"Don't think like that, Emily," George said. "We are not to blame."

"Agreed," Theo said. "You cannot be held accountable for the actions of a grown man capable of making his own decisions." He suddenly took my hand and kissed it, eliciting a polite cough from George. Theo let go, removed his hat, and dashed his fingers through his hair. "My apologies," he muttered.

"No need to apologize," I said, bemused. He was behaving rather oddly all of a sudden. Very...earnest. Perhaps he'd been overcome with ardor. I quite liked the thought of that.

"I wonder what he'll do when he finds his next dose missing?" George said.

A terrible thought struck me. "Will he die without it?"

"No, nothing like that. Having too much of it will kill him, not the withdrawal. Although he'll probably *want* to die as the pain worsens."

"I wonder if this was all he had left." Theo took the package out of his jacket pocket again.

George gasped then half rose out of his seat. He removed his hat, pulled down the window, and shouted at the driver to stop and return to the Institution. We jerked back and forth as the coach halted. The movement sent me closer to Theo. Our thighs touched. Neither of us shifted away.

"I hope we're not too late," George said, his eyes sparkling like gems.

"Too late for what?" Theo asked.

"To follow him," I said, as George's intention became

clear. Excitement trickled down my spine. "If Blunt has no more opium, he will probably go to buy some before his condition worsens. If we can stop him but promise to let him go if he answers our questions, we might finally find out if he is indeed the villain."

"Blackmail." Theo grinned. "Brilliant!"

"I prefer to think of it as an incentive," George said. "Blackmail sounds so despicable and our intentions are honorable."

The coach swung into the traffic and headed back the way we'd come. Within moments it had pulled up outside the school again. Theo got out and spoke to the school's footman. A moment later he returned to the coach and spoke to our driver.

"Blunt did indeed leave just after us," he said as the coach rolled forward. "I've given the driver instructions to slowly scour the nearby streets to search for him. He cannot have gone far."

George looked out one window and I peered out the other. Theo, sitting next to me, reached over my shoulder and lifted the curtain higher. He was so close I could feel his warm breath on my ear and his chest against my back. His heart drummed a strong, rhythmic beat. I liked it. Liked it very much. But I was acutely aware that he wasn't Jacob. I closed my eyes and threw up a prayer that he was all right.

Theo drew in a deep, shuddery breath then shifted back a little. I applauded him for doing the honorable thing, yet part of me missed his solidness, and the way he made my nerves thrum with anticipation.

"I think..." George was off his seat, his nose squashed against the window pane. "There! Getting into that hansom."

"Has he seen us?" I asked. George's coach was distinctive with the Culvert escutcheon painted on the door. Blunt would recognize it instantly.

"I don't think so. By the look of concentration on his face, he's trying not to be sick and doesn't seem to be noticing anything except the cab." He pulled down the window and ordered his driver to follow the hansom but to keep some distance.

"Let's hope they don't travel too fast," I said. "There's an awful lot of traffic. It'll be easy to lose him if your driver is not vigilant."

"I'm not so worried about losing him as I am ending up at an opium den," George said.

Theo murmured agreement. "I've heard some of them are gruesome, certainly unfit for a lady to enter. We must decide who goes in and who stays here with Emily."

"You are not leaving me behind!"

George put up his hands, placating. "Let's worry about that when we find out where he's going. If we can stop him entering the den altogether, we will not need to separate."

I had never seen an opium den before and I wasn't going to see one today. I knew where we were heading as soon as we hit the newer, blander streets of London's outskirts, and it wasn't to a squalid back lane. We drove past houses that were all the same, their features indistinguishable from each other, their facades unassuming.

"He's going to Price's house," I said.

"Leviticus Price?" George screwed up his nose, pushed up his glasses, and squinted at the houses sliding past the window. "Good lord, I think you're right."

"You've mentioned Price before," Theo said. "Is he the paranormal expert?"

"Yes, and now the Grand Master of the Society For Supernatural Activity," George said. "He's very knowledgeable."

"He has helped us in the past," I said. "Albeit reluctantly. He is not the nicest of men."

George snorted. "He's got the manners of a sewer rat. Ah, yes, this is his street."

The coach slowed then pulled to a stop a few houses down from Price's. George poked his head out the window. After a few moments, he pulled it back in. "Price's landlady has just let Blunt inside."

"I wonder why Price has come here and not to a den," I said. "He should be desperate for his opium now. Do you think he's getting it from Price?"

"You may be right," George said.

Theo nodded. "He must be. What a strange arrangement."

"A shocking arrangement," I muttered. "I wonder how long it has been going on."

"Price must be gaining something from it," George said, "but what?"

"Money." Theo's jaw set hard and the word sounded like it was ground between clenched teeth before being spat out. "Why does anyone do anything of a shocking nature?"

I looked to George, but he didn't seem to notice Theo's bitter tirade.

"Let's not condemn Price yet," George said. "We don't know for certain if that's why Blunt has come here. There could be all sorts of other reasons. It could even be a simple social call."

"Oh, George, don't be so naïve," I said. "Price may be the Grand Master of your society, but that doesn't mean he's innocent. For all we know, he may be behind everything."

"Emily! Price may be a little...difficult at times, but he's never abused his paranormal knowledge before."

"That we know of."

"And he did help us find the culprits who released the shape-shifting demon."

"He led us to Finch, who indeed was controlling it, but there was someone else involved too. I am certain of it."

"Blunt."

I shook my head. "I've never been entirely convinced of Blunt's guilt. He was terrified when Jacob haunted him at the school. You'd think a man who knew all about shape-shifting demons would be more comfortable with the supernatural."

"As I recall, Beaufort had a knife. A knife-wielding spirit would terrify anyone."

"Blunt was afraid of being haunted from the start," I said.

"Even before Jacob threatened him with the knife."

George sniffed. "Blunt was the villain then and I am certain he's the villain now too. He must be. Look at him. Any man in the grip of opium must have a guilty conscience to suppress."

"Any man controlled by opium is too weak of mind to be behind the summoning of Mortlock and now this curse. Price has proven to us on many occasion that he is very strong willed."

"It cannot be Price," George said. "He doesn't have children and his name is not Seymour."

"The same can be said of Blunt, yet you consider him the villain."

George said nothing to that, probably because whatever argument he used would also throw suspicion on Price. Instead, he opened the coach door.

"Let's go and see what they're up to, shall we?"

Theo caught his arm. "I don't think that's a good idea. We don't want to alert them to our suspicions."

George sat back with a sigh and shut the door again. "We need Jacob."

They both looked to me. "He's terribly unwell," I said, then I realized how absurd it was for a spirit to be described as ill. "I don't want to summon him. I think we should wait a little longer."

"What if they're putting a curse on the Otherworld right at this moment?" George said. "We should go in."

"You're right." Another curse might spell the end for both Jacob and the Waiting Area. "Let's go."

"It will serve to eliminate Price, if nothing else."

Theo shook his head and stayed me with a hand to my arm. "I don't think Blunt would be in any state right now to enter the Otherworld, or assist Price to."

"I give you that point," George said, sitting back down. "Once he takes the opium, he'll be useless for a while."

So we waited. And waited. George's stomach growled every minute, without fail. It was mid-afternoon and we'd not had luncheon.

"My apologies," he said after each gurgle.

I rubbed my temples where a dull ache had taken up residence, tapping against my skull. "Perhaps we should go. Nothing is happening here."

Jacob appeared on the seat beside George but I could see right through him. He slumped forward, resting his elbows on his knees, and looked up at me through tired, flat eyes.

"Jacob." I stifled a sob. "Oh, Jacob."

George and Theo followed my gaze.

Jacob held up a hand as if to assure me he was fine, but it was unconvincing considering the look of him. "You're right," he said, his voice thin. "Nothing will happen here now."

"You've been inside?"

He nodded. "Briefly. Blunt is lying dazed on Price's sofa. He's an opium addict."

"We know. We found a small amount on his person. What about Price? What was he doing?"

"Reading the newspaper near the fireplace."

"So he supplied Blunt with the opium." I relayed the details of Jacob's account to Theo and George.

George blew out a breath. "I suppose you're right. I cannot believe it. Leviticus Price, an opium supplier."

"Emily, I have to...go." Jacob faded away and I thought that was it, he'd gone, but he returned, albeit faintly.

My heart jumped into my throat. I wanted to hold him, but that wasn't possible with an audience and he looked much too ethereal to grasp anyway. "Go if you must. Rest."

He weakened again, only to flare up, as if he'd used some energy he'd kept in reserve. "There's...I need to...you..." His words faded in and out with his body.

"You need to tell me something?"

He nodded. "Mrs. White..."

"Yes, you said Seymour earlier. Is she related to Frederick in some way?"

He lifted one shoulder in a shrug. "I found...type."

"You found a type? Type of what?"

With a frustrated click of his tongue, he became as solid as he used to be. "Daguerreotype."

"You found a daguerreotype in her room?"

He nodded. "It was of Mrs. White and a young man. I recognized him."

My knees bumped his. I had not known I was leaning forward. Theo and George leaned forward too even though they could not hear Jacob.

"Frederick," I said on a whisper. "It was Frederick in the picture, wasn't it?"

"The one I fought," Jacob said with a nod. He began to fade again at an alarming rate.

"Do you think they are related?"

"Yes. It...family portrait."

I pressed my hand to my mouth. It was too strange, too amazing. Just as I was about to ask more questions, Jacob disappeared. He did not come back.

"What is it?" George asked.

"Emily, are you all right?" Theo frowned at me. "You look quite pale."

"Mrs. White," I blurted out. I told them about the daguerreotype in her room. "To have a portrait of just her and Frederick, that must mean they are, or were, very close."

"His mother?" George said. "Surely not."

"What do we know of her?" Theo asked.

"Very little," I said. "Your cousin, Wallace, told us Frederick lived with his father. Wallace assumed the mother had died until one day Frederick told him she was very much alive. He never did find out what happened to her."

"So Mrs. White is cursing the Otherworld?" George stuck his head out of the window and called instructions to return to the Grosvenor Street house.

"It is certainly looking that way." The coach moved off. I thought George was about to say "I told you it wasn't Price," but he caught my glare and shut his mouth.

"What will we say to her when we see her?" Theo asked.

"We cannot accuse her of being Mrs. Seymour without proof."

"The daguerreotype will be proof," George said.

"But we cannot enter her room if she refuses to let us in."

"Theo's right," I said. "But I think there's another way. George, tell your driver to divert to my house."

George banged on the roof of the coach then shouted the order out the window. "Don't keep us in suspense, Em," he said when he sat back in the seat. "What have you in mind?"

"Do you recall how the shape-shifting demon escaped?"

"Your sister accidentally released it."

Theo laughed then quickly apologized. "But it does sound rather ridiculous. How does one *accidentally* release a demon?"

I told him of the peddler woman who'd come to our house and convinced Celia to purchase a rather interesting amulet to use as a prop at our séances. When I'd summoned the spirit at our next event, she'd used the amulet in what she'd assumed was a harmless manner and the demon had emerged through the open portal.

"I see," Theo said. "If the person cursing the Otherworld is the same as the one who released the demon and Mortlock, then the peddler is our prime suspect."

"And my sister might recognize her."

"Which is why you need her to see Mrs. White," George finished.

"Didn't she meet Mrs. White when she worked at the school?" Theo asked.

"No, she only dealt with Blunt."

"Brilliant move, Emily," George said. "You're exceedingly clever for a woman." He knew he'd said something wrong as soon as it was out of his mouth. I didn't even need to glare at him, although I did anyway. "I, uh, my apologies. That's not what I meant."

"It most certainly is what you meant," I said.

Theo snorted a laugh.

"I don't see the funny side," I snapped at him.

"No?" Theo nodded at George. "Just look at his face. Any moment now he'll get down on his knees and beg forgiveness."

George did look terribly upset so I stopped glaring.

"I am sorry and you must believe me when I say I didn't mean it to sound the way it did. You and Adelaide are the cleverest females I've met. She could match wits with the most learned of paranormal scholars. She's very easy to teach, takes everything in. I admire her greatly."

"So I see," I said dryly. Listening to him back-pedal made me think of Jacob. Now *he* would never have slighted the whole of womankind.

Theo nudged me with his elbow. "Never mind. I still admire *you* greatly." His eyes twinkled mischievously. "Shall I list all your virtues to make you feel better?"

"We haven't enough time for that. The ride home is only ten minutes."

He chuckled. "I do admire you though, Emily. You are a most remarkable woman."

"And you are much too kind."

"I wouldn't say that." The twinkle vanished, but he continued to watch me from beneath his long lashes. It was most unnerving. I couldn't begin to guess what was meant by his unexpected intensity. His earlier humor was gone, and the adoration with it, which was rather peculiar, not to mention disappointing. He seemed...disturbed by something.

I chatted incessantly all the way home to distract myself. By the time we arrived in Druids Way, I couldn't recall what I'd said. Something about Adelaide's ball.

It wasn't as easy to convince Celia to come with us as I thought it would be. She refused to leave until we'd all had a quick bite to eat.

"You haven't eaten all day," she said, setting down the letter she was reading on the table beside the sofa. She rose and pulled the bell cord to summon Lucy. "Think of the men. They cannot be expected to work on an empty stomach."

I looked up at the ceiling in the hope of finding some patience there. "Celia, forget about food, this is important."

"It can wait." Lucy arrived and Celia gave orders to serve cold meat, bread and cheese in the dining room. "And take something out for the driver and footmen too."

"Celia! We must go!"

"Actually, Em," George said, "I'm exceedingly hungry."

"We'll eat quickly," Theo assured me.

"And the horses could do with a rest," George went on. "I'll have the driver give them some feed while they wait."

He left, as did Celia to help Lucy. I sat on the sofa and picked up the letter my sister had been reading. My stomach sank as I read.

"Something wrong?" Theo asked, sitting next to me, his hat in his hands.

"Another cancelation."

"Ah."

"You and George were right. My reputation is in tatters and our business on the brink of ruin." I had never liked conducting the séances, but I'd never actually thought a time would come when we didn't do them. It was all rather sudden and not quite real.

His fingers edged around the brim of his hat. "I'm sorry, Emily. I'm truly sorry." He looked at the hat, not at me.

"Thank you, but *you* don't need to apologize. It's not your fault."

"No, of course not." He looked up at me and his blond hair flopped over his eyes. He seemed much older all of a sudden, and very serious. "I just don't like seeing you in difficulty."

"It's no difficulty. Celia will have some money saved. She always does."

"What do I always do?" she asked, coming back into the drawing room.

"Have money saved." I indicated the letter. "Another

cancelation, I see."

She nodded, grim. "That's the sixth I've received today."

"Sixth!" Good lord. So many. "You do have money set aside, don't you, Celia?" If she didn't, the letter could have just thrust us into what Theo politely labeled 'difficulty.' It was more like poverty. We could not hope to support ourselves without a steady income.

"Not now, Emily, we have a guest." She held out her hand to Theo and he rose and offered his arm. "Luncheon won't be long."

It seemed discussions about our financial state would have to wait a little longer.

When we finally all piled into the carriage again, it was late afternoon. The hazy ball that was the sun had not yet sunk below the buildings, but cast long shadows across the road. Traffic was light and Grosvenor Street not far, but far enough for us to form a plan on the way.

When we arrived at number twelve, Celia and I went down to the servants' entrance below street level. I asked for Mrs. White and as with our last visit, we were shown into the tiny drawing room. She arrived a few minutes later, a polite but strained smile on her face.

"How can I help you, Miss Chambers?"

"This is my sister, Miss Celia Chambers, " I said.

The two women gave each other polite nods, but Mrs. White didn't offer a smile. "Is there something I can do for you both?"

"Oh no, this is a social call," I said. "We were in the area, you see, and when I told my sister about you, she asked to meet you."

"I'm very flattered, and I don't mean to seem ungracious, but I'm very busy. Perhaps another time?"

"Yes, of course," I said.

Celia rose. "What a shame. I was looking forward to a little chat. Emily has spoken so highly of you."

The whole exchange lasted not even a minute. Mrs. White saw us out, apologized again, then shut the door.

"Is she always that rude?" Celia said.

We headed back to the carriage, parked on the other side of Grosvenor Square. We had not wanted Mrs. White to see it. Even if she happened to look out of the top floor window, she could not possibly pick out George's Clarence among the sea of black coaches. She was too far away for one thing, and the tall trees in the central square would block her view.

"Do you think she's aware we're suspicious of her?" I asked.

"She has no reason to be, does she?"

"I don't think so. Well, you had a long enough look at her. Was she the peddler?"

Celia shrugged and walked a few paces along the path before answering. "I don't know."

I stopped and forced her to halt alongside me. "What do you mean? How can you not know?"

"Hush, Emily." Celia gave a polite smile to an elegantly dressed gentleman walking past. He doffed his hat but did not meet her gaze. "Oh, why didn't I take a better look at the peddler!"

"You have no inkling one way or another?"

"None. I could not see a likeness between Mrs. White and the peddler, but if she were disguised with a wig and ragged clothing..." She shook her head. "It's no excuse. I feel utterly useless."

"Never mind. I doubt I would have taken much notice either."

She put her arm around my shoulders. "I used to recall the day when I would be the one reassuring you." She tucked a strand of loose hair behind my ear. "You've grown up so much lately. No wonder Louis is taken with you."

"Is he?" I hadn't expected her to speak of Louis. She seemed to dislike him so. But now that she had, I wanted to grasp the conversation with both hands. I deliberately slowed my pace to allow us more time. "Celia, what does he think of me?"

"I'm sure he cannot fail to see how clever and courageous you are."

"Really?" It warmed my heart to hear her say it. "I do like him. He seems very nice, and noble. He saved a man's life. Imagine that!"

"Yes. Imagine." We strolled a little more in silence until she suddenly stopped. We were almost at the fence on the other side of the square. The coach was within sight. George stood nearby, watching us, but Theo was a little apart, chatting to two ladies with their backs to us. "Emily...this pains me to say it, but...please be careful with Louis. He's not proven that he can be a good father."

"I don't think I need a father at seventeen. Indeed, I've never had one until now. I'll be happy just to see him on occasion and be friends."

"You won't be able to see him. He's going back to Victoria soon."

"I haven't forgotten." I walked off, my heart in my throat. My own reaction to Louis' pending departure surprised me.

Celia took my arm again. I sensed she had more to say but was holding back for some reason.

"Well?" George asked, standing aside so the footman could open the door. Theo joined us, the ladies having walked off. "Was Mrs. White the peddler?"

Celia lowered her head. "I don't know. I'm sorry. I've disappointed everyone."

We piled into the carriage and took our seats, the men opposite my sister and me.

"I say we confront her," George said. "Tell her we know she's Frederick's mother and we know what she's doing to Beaufort and the Waiting Area."

"We can't," I said.

"I agree with Emily," Theo said. "Mrs. White cannot be the one delivering the curses. To die and then return to life requires a period of recovery. She couldn't work as a governess at the same time. Her employer would know."

"She may be helping whoever it is then," George said.

"Or at the very least, she may know who it is."

"Still, I don't want to confront her," I said. "It's too soon. We don't know enough. Let's watch her for now. As soon as she leaves the house, we'll follow her."

"*You* will do no such thing, Emily," Celia said.

"But I must!"

"No, you must not. It's late and you could be here for some time. All night, possibly. I don't think even I need to remind you of the proper rules of conduct. Even a half-wit should understand you would break every last one if you remained here with these two gentlemen in the dark."

"Then what do you propose this half-wit do?"

Theo cleared his throat. "Might I offer a suggestion? Culvert and I will stay and watch."

"Excellent idea!" George said. "Hyde, you remain behind while I take the ladies home. I'll stop by my house for a change of horses and driver. We won't need footmen." His eyes lit up and he looked like a child about to experience his first Christmas. "Cook should have something set aside that we can eat cold for dinner. Chicken pie, perhaps. How does that sound, Hyde?"

"Delicious," Theo said. "And something sweet for afterwards?"

"Of course. I'll bring fresh shirts for the morning and blankets for tonight too."

"I don't suppose you could put in a flask of whiskey."

"One flask won't get us far, I'll make it two large ones."

"It isn't a house party," I said, laughing. It was impossible not to get caught up in their excitement. "You're not supposed to have fun."

George grinned. "I'm rather looking forward to it. I'll tell Mother I've gone to my club, and I'll have word sent to your aunt too, Hyde."

"What about your studies, Mr. Hyde?" Celia asked. "Don't you have classes in the morning?"

"This is far more important," Theo said. "Culvert can't do it alone. Let me worry about my studies, Miss Chambers."

It was settled. Celia, George, and I drove off, while Theo remained in Grosvenor Square, looking across Grosvenor Street to number twelve.

It was going to be a long night for them, and perhaps a long one for me too, lying awake and wondering how they fared. I was prepared for it. I was not prepared, however, to be greeted by a faint ghost, a cross father, and a guilty looking little girl upon my return.

CHAPTER 8

"I'm sorry," Cara blurted out as George's coach drove off. "It's all my fault."

"What's all your fault?" Celia asked.

Louis scowled at my sister. She scowled back. "Cara thinks she can see ghosts," he said.

"I can!" She clamped a hand over her mouth and her wide eyes begged for forgiveness, but I wasn't sure whose forgiveness she wanted.

"It's my fault," Jacob said, rubbing a hand through his hair, messing it up. He seemed to be pausing for breath, but that was impossible. He didn't need to breathe. "I startled her...he was here." He chucked Cara under the chin. "Don't worry."

"But he thinks I'm mad," she whispered, even though Louis would have heard.

"I think we should go inside," Celia said, leading the way.

Louis watched her stiff back, his frown deepening. "Don't tell me you allow her to believe this nonsense. Celia, I'm surprised at you."

I heard Celia suck air between her teeth, but she kept walking and said nothing. It must have been hard for her not to confront him then and there. I had to bite my tongue to stop myself telling him Cara could indeed see spirits, as could I. But some things ought not be revealed on front doorsteps.

Nobody spoke until we were settled in the drawing room. Lucy had collected our hats and coats and hung them up then trotted off to the kitchen to make tea.

"Mr. Moreau," Celia began, "I think—"

"It's Louis to you, Celia. After everything we've been through, don't you think you can cease the formality?"

"Formality and manners are all we have left, *Mr.* Moreau."

"Very well, *Celia*, if that's how you want to be. I see I cannot change your mind."

"No, you cannot. Now, what I'm about to tell you, may shock you."

"I doubt anything can shock me after learning I have a seventeen year-old daughter." He winked at me and I smiled back, despite my reservations.

Jacob came up beside me and sat on the arm of the sofa. Ordinarily he liked to stand, but he seemed to need the rest. I desperately wanted to ask him if many spirits had been lost from the Waiting Area, and if he was all right to carry on being in this realm, but I did not. One crisis at a time.

"Cara can see spirits," Celia said, rather more bluntly than necessary. If she'd let me speak first, I would have gently steered the conversation in that direction in a way that would not have stunned Louis into silence.

His jaw worked and a muscle high up in his cheek twitched. He took a long time to answer, and when he did, he spoke as if every word were carefully chosen. "I don't think it's wise to take this path, Celia."

"What path?"

"The path of..." His gaze darted to Cara, who sat like a little statue, pretending not to hear her elders talking about her. "Of pretending she's normal. I've seen madness. My father is...touched by it. You've met him." His tone was neutral, but a hint of sadness underpinned it.

Celia scoffed. "You're comparing that crazy old Frenchman with these two?"

Louis' gaze caught mine and I was shocked by what I saw there. Genuine, raw sorrow. "Emily too?"

He was not going to be easy to convince. "Celia, wait." I held up my hand. "Let me do this. Louis, we haven't been entirely honest with you because, well, we were afraid of your reaction."

"Don't be," he said. "You can tell me anything, Emily, even if it's...something unfortunate."

"And the same goes for you. You can tell us anything."

"Ah. I see." He folded his arms over his chest. "You wish to bargain with me?" His low chuckle surprised me, coming so soon after the sadness.

"We'll offer explanations, but only if you promise to do the same after we've finished."

"I admire your methods, Emily. I shouldn't, but I do."

"As do I," Jacob said. He clutched my shoulder, but I suspect it was more to steady himself than for affectionate reasons.

"Jacob?" I whispered. "Are you all right?"

"Don't worry." His smile was weak but heartfelt.

"Who are you speaking to?" Louis asked.

Celia huffed out an exasperated breath. "You heard her, Mr. Moreau. We give you no answers until you promise."

He gave a single nod. "Very well. I promise. But you first. So tell me. When did this madness—"

"It's not madness," Celia said. "Emily and Cara can see spirits. Thanks to you, I might add."

"What are you talking about? Or are you mad too?"

Her glare could have cut glass. "Only at you."

"Stop it," I said. "You two are worse than children."

Louis apologized and looked ashamed. My sister did not. "*Now*, will someone please explain what is going on?" he asked.

"Allow me," Jacob said. He picked up a figurine of an Oriental lady from a nearby table. His movements were slow, as if his limbs were heavy.

Louis leapt out of his chair. "Bloody hell!"

"I really don't think that sort of language is necessary," Celia scolded.

"My, uh, my...sorry. I'm..." He sat back down, slowly, without taking his gaze off the figurine. "What trickery is this?"

"It's not trickery," I said. "It's Jacob Beaufort, son of Lord and Lady Preston. Or rather, his spirit."

"He's dead," Cara said. "Only me and Emily can see him."

"Emily and I," Celia corrected.

"But..." Louis said. "But...I don't understand."

Lucy entered carrying a tray and tea things. She paused when she saw the figurine. "Mr. Beaufort is here?" She set the tray on the table near Celia. "I always feel that I should be offering him tea since he is our guest."

Jacob lowered the figurine onto the table. "Emily...I must go." He pressed his hands to his temples. "But I need to speak to you." He dropped to his knees in front of me. Exhaustion raked at his features, dragging them down, aging him. He pressed his forehead against my knees and sighed deeply. "Emily, I may not...return."

"No!"

"What is it?" Louis asked, half out of the chair again. "What's wrong?"

"He's saying goodbye," Cara said softly. "Mr. Beaufort is sick."

"Isn't he already dead?"

"Jacob," I whispered, shutting them out. "Jacob, we'll stop whoever it is. Trust me. We've made progress, thanks to you. George and Theo are watching Mrs. White and we're sure she'll lead us to the culprit."

He lifted his head to peer up at me. "I know...must go...can't stay."

"Will someone please tell me what is happening?" Louis said.

I touched Jacob's semi-transparent cheek and he leaned into my palm. Then he was gone.

I fought back tears. *It's not goodbye, it's not goodbye.* If I kept chanting that in my head, perhaps I might believe it.

"Actually, Emily, I agree with Mr. Moreau," Celia said. "You must keep me informed. What is Mr. Beaufort saying?"

"Nothing," I said. "He's gone."

"You believe this is all real, don't you?" Louis said. I thought he was talking to me, but he was looking at Celia.

"She can see spirits," Lucy said, puffing out her considerable chest. She handed Louis a teacup and saucer. "She talks to them all the time. Miss Cara too. But there's no need to be afraid. Most are harmless. I used to be afraid, but not anymore."

"Thank you, Lucy," Celia said. "You may go."

Lucy bobbed a curtsey and left.

My sister picked up her cup. "If you spend long enough with Emily or Cara, you will discover that it's not an illusion."

"But it must be!"

Celia sighed. "Have you ever known me to be prone to flights of fancy? If you say yes, then you don't know me at all, Louis."

He watched her from beneath his thick, black lashes for so long, I began to feel uncomfortable. Cara wriggled in her seat, her cup of chocolate held close to her chest as if she were protecting it.

"You called me Louis," he finally said.

"A slip of the tongue." Celia sipped.

"Cara and I can both communicate with spirits," I said. I felt like I was intruding on something private, but I couldn't put my finger on what. Celia and Louis weren't even looking at each other. "It's a family trait," I added. "Inherited from you and your father."

Louis whipped round to face me. "If that were the case, then I should be able to see spirits too. Or Papa."

"Only the women can, but the men are the ones who

102

pass it along to their daughters. You don't have aunts on your father's side, do you?"

"No. My father is an only child." He frowned. "I think you need to tell me everything, Emily."

I did. I started with what I'd learned in George's books about our ancestry. By the time I'd finished, I'd told him all about Jacob's death, the shape-shifting demon, Mortlock's possession, and the curse on the Waiting Area. I did not tell him how my life had been in danger on numerous occasions. Not even Celia was aware of everything I'd been up to in the past few weeks.

He sat there, unblinking, saying nothing, and we three did not push him. We sat and sipped and waited. At first I was unsure if he'd believe me, but after several minutes I could see he did. He would not look so worried if he did not.

Celia cracked first. "Well?" she asked, shrilly. "Do you still think your own sister and daughter are mad?"

"Celia, that's not fair," I said.

But Louis did not look offended. "If it weren't for you, Celia, I might. I'm sorry, Emily, Cara, but I know neither of you as well as I know Celia. As she said, she's not prone to fanciful thoughts. If she says you can see ghosts, then I must believe that you can."

Celia put her cup to her lips even though I knew she'd finished her tea some time ago. Her eyelids were lowered, so I could not see her eyes, but I distinctly heard her sniff.

"Thank you," I said. My relief surprised me. I hadn't thought I cared so much for his good opinion.

"Tell me what I can do to help," he said. "This villain...the one cursing the Otherworld...he must be stopped."

"Emily will stop him," Cara said.

"My friends, George and Theo, are watching the house of a suspect tonight, "I said. "I'll see them in the morning and find out if she went anywhere. There's little else to do. But thank you."

"Friends...is that all these gentlemen are to you?"

Celia clicked her tongue. "Honestly, Mr. Moreau, it's a little late to be coming across as fatherly now."

"Celia," I hissed. "Stop it."

Louis merely shrugged. He looked at his teacup, which he'd set down on the tray. He hadn't touched it. Perhaps he didn't drink tea. There was so much about my father I was yet to learn. "I suppose it's my turn now." When none of us spoke, he continued. "I went to New South Wales on a government scheme. I didn't want to be assistant to my father forever, and there aren't many opportunities for a man like me in England."

I could well imagine. My skin was light compared to my father's. Whereas I was sometimes called exotic, he would have been labeled much worse. We didn't press him for details and he gave none.

"I wanted to prove I was worthy of your mother," he said to me. "She was...very proper, you see. I thought...I thought that if I couldn't be a gentleman here in London, then I could be a wealthy man in another country. My plan was to earn enough money in New South Wales then write to you both and have you join me," he said to Celia.

"We...she...never wanted you to leave," Celia said. "How can you expect us to uproot our lives to follow to the other side of the world?"

"When you love someone, anything is possible. But only if you truly want to be with them."

Celia turned away to stare at the fireplace.

"What happened?" I asked. "Why didn't you write?"

"Making my fortune proved more difficult than I imagined. Work paid little. I could never save enough. I was ashamed of my failure, so I didn't write. I didn't want anyone to know that I'd amounted to precisely nothing. Especially her."

"You should have," I said. "She would not have thought you a failure. Not if she loved you."

"Whether she did or not...it doesn't matter now. As the years passed, I came to regret my decision of not writing.

Regret it deeply." He cast a glance at Celia, but she didn't move, didn't look at him. She sat stiff and proud, staring into the fireplace. "But I was young at the time, and I thought I'd be a disappointment."

"Nonsense," I said. "Anyway, as it turned out, you're quite successful. You said your shop is doing very well."

"It is. Now. But I've only had it two years."

"And before that you worked in low-paying jobs?"

"At the beginning, for a year. It was around that time that I'd decided I had to write to your mother regardless of my poor state. I missed her. Missed her keenly," he said softly. "I had never told her how much, and after so long without her, I knew I needed to tell her how I felt and let her make up her own mind."

"What happened to change your mind?" I asked. "Why didn't you write then?"

"You met another woman," Celia said. "It's understandable. You must have been lonely."

"There was no one else. Never, ever anyone else."

Celia's breath hitched, but only I could have heard it.

"I didn't write because my situation grew worse. I went to prison."

"Prison!" Cara and I cried in unison.

Celia's cup fell to the floor. It was empty, fortunately, but she did not move to retrieve it. I picked it up and set it on the table. She'd gone quite pale.

"If I wasn't a failure before, then I was certainly one then. How could I support a wife from prison? How could I ever face her? I decided writing would have to wait. Indeed, I admit that I lost all hope of ever seeing your mother again. I was determined to give her up and I hoped she would forget me in time. It was for the best."

"She never did," I said, but I wasn't sure what was in my mother's heart. She'd never spoken of Louis. If anything, she seemed more in love with Celia's father as the years wore on. Poor Louis. Pining for a woman who did not care for him as much as he cared for her. Such a tragedy and a waste.

"What did you do to be sent to prison?" I asked.

"I was in the wrong place at the wrong time. A riot started at a mine where I worked. Conditions were terrible and the pay poor. Many resented it and some decided to take action one night after drinking too much. They stormed the manager's office, broke windows and furniture, and stole some of the gold. Although I didn't participate, I was nearby when it happened, and was identified."

"How could they identify you when you didn't do anything?"

He shrugged. "That's the way it is when these things happen. Whenever there's chaos, witnesses become unreliable."

"Why didn't you fight the charge?" Celia cried. Tears shone in her eyes, but I'd wager they were tears of anger and frustration, because those were precisely the emotions warring within me.

"How can you be so...so calm about it all?" I asked.

Louis shrugged again. "Sydney's justice system is worse than London's. The wheels grind slowly, and a witness is a witness. I could not prove I *wasn't* there, so his testimony stood. It's not his fault. He had no malicious intent. It was an honest mistake and I've forgiven him for it. Especially considering whom I met in jail. It wasn't all bad in the end."

"Don't keep us in suspense!" I said when he didn't go on.

He smiled. "I met Harry in prison. He was the man who would become my business partner. We became good friends, perhaps because we were both innocent. Harry was wrongly convicted of theft by his own brother-in-law. In his case, the witness was malicious and deliberately gave false evidence. His brother-in-law wanted Harry out of the way so he could manage their joint business and reap all the profit. They had a large shop in the center of Sydney where they sold all sorts of things from haberdashery to groceries. When we both completed our jail terms, we decided to leave Sydney and start a similar shop in Melbourne in the south. That was two years ago and I return to London a prosperous man now."

"And a free one," I said, grinning. "Goodness, what a tale! Oh, what about the time you saved a man's life? Was that Harry?"

"Ah, that," he said, turning gloomy. "There was another prisoner with us who wasn't on good terms with anyone." He glanced at Cara and I suspected he was tempering his story for her sake. "Harry accidentally knocked the other prisoner's plate over during mealtime. He set upon Harry and would have killed him if I hadn't stepped in. The prisoner died some hours later in the infirmary from his injuries." He lowered his head. "That's another thing I've regretted every day since," he said quietly.

"But it was in self-defense."

"It still weighs heavily on my conscience."

"I'm sure your friend is glad you were there," Celia murmured. "You should not regret an action that saves another, better man. Emily called you noble." She lifted her chin. "I agree with her."

"Thank you. That means more to me than...well, than most things."

"I have a very brave brother," Cara said. "Tell me more about New South Wales. Is it very wild?"

"Much of it, yes. Victoria too. That's the colony in the south where I live now. Melbourne is its main center and a bustling, lively place it is these days. There is so much vibrancy there, so much hope. You can see it in the new buildings going up all over the place and in the eyes of the people too. I would love you to see it. All of you."

"Can we go, Celia?" Cara said. "Can we? Pleeeease."

"Absolutely not! The colonies are on the other side of the world. The voyage alone could kill you."

"Celia," Louis said, "don't dampen her enthusiasm. The voyage is not so bad if you can afford a decent cabin on the ship. And I can afford it."

Celia stood and held her hand out to Cara. "Don't be ridiculous. Our lives are here. No one is moving to the end of the world. London suits us perfectly. We have a thriving business of our own here and we cannot abandon it."

The strain in her voice was faint, but it was there. I doubted Louis would have heard it, not knowing that our business was in trouble. I certainly did, loud and clear.

"Come, girls, time for dinner. Good night, Mr. Moreau."

I gave Louis an apologetic wince. "I tend to agree with Celia," I said. "Our lives are here."

"There's nothing for us there." Celia might as well have driven the point home with a blunt axe, so brutal were her words.

I am there, Louis might have said. But he did not. He stood and gave a shallow bow. "I won't keep you from your dinner. Good night, ladies." He let himself out.

Celia waited for the sound of the front door closing then walked off, her strides long and purposeful. I thought she'd gone to the dining room, but when Cara and I entered, she wasn't there.

"Why won't she even think about going to New South Wales or Victoria or wherever it is?" Cara asked. "She didn't even let him tell us about his house or nothing!"

"I don't know." My sister was certainly not herself to behave so rudely to a guest. "Perhaps she's still upset on Mama's behalf. Louis did leave her behind, with no word, and now she's gone he can never make amends."

Lucy entered carrying a tureen. "Mr. Moreau didn't stay for dinner?"

"No."

"I wish he were my father," Cara said. "Then I'd go with him to the colonies."

I kissed her forehead. "Then I would miss you greatly, my little aunt."

***

It was difficult not to summon Jacob. I desperately wanted to know if he was still in the Waiting Area. But part of me was too afraid of discovering that he was not, and the other part was afraid that summoning him would weaken him. I couldn't bear it if I were the cause of further pain, yet I could hardly bear not seeing him.

It was a hint of how the rest of my life would be. Alone. Jacob gone forever, never to return.

I did not like it.

George arrived in the morning to take me back to Grosvenor Street where he'd left Theo watching the house. He looked like he hadn't slept in a week, rather than just one night. His clothes were crumpled, his jaw lined with stubble and his eyes red-rimmed.

"Oh George," I said on a sigh. "Spending the night in the coach wasn't quite as much fun as you'd hoped, was it?"

He removed his glasses and squeezed the bridge of his nose. "It was a living nightmare. I froze to death, my left leg went numb, and I cannot turn my head further than..." He turned to the right and winced. "Further than that. To top it off, Hyde slept like a baby. He snores, by the way. I think that's something you should know if you're planning on marrying him."

I tried to stifle a laugh but it escaped as a snort. "How fortunate that you're a gentleman and not a woodsman or soldier. You would be quite miserable sleeping out of doors or in a tent." I leaned across the gap between us and fixed his crooked necktie. "You cannot even dress yourself."

He stretched his neck out of his collar. "Thank you. I admit I'm lost without my valet."

"So did anything happen? Did Mrs. White leave the house?"

"No. I wish she had. The excitement would have given us something to do. As it was, we were bored out of our minds. Well, I was. Hyde managed to sleep for hours."

We arrived at Grosvenor Square on the opposite side to Grosvenor Street so as not to be seen. Dew glistened on leaves and grass as the sun peeped demurely through the gaps between the buildings in the east. Carts rattled past, stopping at each house to make deliveries or for the driver to talk to the maids sweeping the steps. There were no ladies or gentlemen out at such an early hour. Only those with work to do had to be up early, and the owners of the houses surrounding Grosvenor Square did not need to work.

Our carriage pulled up near Theo. He leaned against the fence enclosing Grosvenor Square, his arms and ankles crossed, his gaze intent on number twelve just visible through the trees. The laconic pose suited his boyish handsomeness and my stomach did a little dip when he saw me and smiled. To think, he was courting *me*, a nobody with a very un-English heritage and strange line of trade.

"Good morning," he said, climbing into the carriage. He rubbed his gloved hands together and eyed the basket I'd set beside me. "If that's what I think it is, I'll have to kiss you, Emily Chambers."

"Steady on," George warned.

"It's Lucy's doing," I said. "Perhaps you should kiss her."

"I'll kiss Culvert if there's hot tea in there."

"Lucky George." I lifted the cloth covering the basket and pulled out a teapot that Lucy had packed firmly into the corner so it wouldn't move. "There is indeed warm tea. And bread, cheese, and cold beef."

The two men ate their breakfast as if they'd never tasted anything so good, while I watched the house. The gap in the trees gave me the perfect view of the wide colonnaded façade, including the entrance to the basement service area. If Mrs. White left the house without her charges, she would exit that way.

By mid-morning, the sun had burned off the dew. George slept quietly in the corner, his glasses in his lap. I told Theo about my evening with my father without taking my gaze off the mansion.

"I'm glad he accepted your...talent," he said. "I know how important it is to you."

"It is, and he did, thank goodness. I'm not sure how I would have reacted if he'd been more like Lord Preston."

"Your father seems like quite the remarkable man."

"That's not all." I told him how Louis had been to jail,

saved a man's life, and was now a successful businessman in Melbourne. "He's made something of himself there. I'm very pleased for him."

When he didn't answer me, I turned to look at him. "What is it?"

"I...I was simply wondering if you were thinking of returning to Melbourne with him."

"No! Of course not. I couldn't leave London."

He flicked his fingernail with his thumb, over and over, a nervous habit he seemed to have just acquired. "Not even if your business fails?"

"It won't fail. It can't. I won't consider it."

George sat up at that moment and rubbed his eyes. "Wh...what's happened?" He fumbled for his glasses and put them on. "Is Mrs. White leaving?" He squinted through the window. "Good lord, look who it is!"

"Who?" I asked, peering past him.

"Miss Beaufort." He fiddled with his tie, smoothed down his hair, and clapped his hat on his head. "How do I look?"

Like he hadn't been home all night. "Very handsome. Is she alone?"

"Her mother is with her." He opened the door and greeted them. I climbed out behind him, Theo at my heels.

We exchanged pleasantries and since George had gone all quiet, it was left to me to explain why we were loafing in the carriage at Grosvenor Square.

"She's in number twelve, you say?" Lady Preston said when I'd finished. "That's Lord and Lady Montgomery's house."

"You know them?"

"Quite well. This Mrs. White...you truly think she's Mrs. Seymour?"

"Jacob is convinced of it, as am I. I wish she'd make a move today. This waiting is very hard on our nerves. Well, it's been harder on Theo and George. They've been here all night."

"All night!" Adelaide took a step closer to George and

raised her hand as if she would touch the stubble on his chin, but she did not. Her mother cleared her throat, and Adelaide's fist returned to her side. She looked down at her walking boots.

George's face turned red and he made a great show of watching the mansion. Theo seemed not to be aware of the conversation at all. He was staring into the distance at a group of ladies clustered at the corner.

"It's been quite some weeks since I've visited Lady Montgomery," Lady Preston said. "I think it's time I paid her a call." She stamped the point of her parasol onto the road. "I have a sudden interest in governesses. Come, Adelaide." Lady Preston walked off, using her parasol as a walking stick, not that she needed a crutch. "Our other call can wait."

Adelaide pulled a face. "I'm supposed to be seeing Bertie and the Duchess of Sandridge," she whispered to us. "Talking about governesses will be far more entertaining." She trotted after her mother, glancing over her shoulder at George twice.

He sighed. "She looks particularly lovely today. That jacket is very fetching on her neat figure and I do like the addition of all those ruffles."

"I had no idea you were an admirer of ladies fashion," I teased.

"Only the fashion of one particular lady." His blush deepened.

"Will you two excuse me for the rest of the day," Theo suddenly said. He sounded distracted, and I don't think he'd heard any of the conversation. "I seem to have developed a slight headache, and I have classes to attend today."

"Oh. Yes. Of course," I said. "You mustn't miss any more lectures. We'll manage without you."

He took my hand and bowed over it. "Good luck, and be careful. Culvert, I'm relying on you to protect her if necessary."

"Never fear," George said with a deep breath that puffed out his chest. "I packed the dueling pistols. They're under the seat."

Theo clapped him on the shoulder, bowed again to me, then strolled off. George and I returned to the carriage and waited.

A while later, Lady Preston and Adelaide climbed in alongside us. The elder sat down, her blue eyes hard and flat, her fingers rigid around the stem of her parasol.

It was Adelaide who spoke, however, her voice rising with excitement. "You will *never* believe what we learned about Mrs. White."

CHAPTER 9

"Do not leave us in suspense!" I cried. "What did you learn?"

Adelaide's face was flushed, her eyes shining as if in a fever. "Mrs. White was a nurse."

The hairs on the back of my neck stood up. I didn't know the particulars of how the person speaking the curse was being brought back to life, but I did know it was possible for someone with the right medical training to do it.

"She was a nurse at St. Thomas's Hospital before she married. That's one of the main reasons Lady Montgomery hired her. One of her girls is sickly, you see, and having a trained nurse in the house eases her mind."

"Good lord." George rubbed his stubbly chin thoughtfully.

"Her guilt is beyond doubt." The quiet steel in Lady Preston's voice drew our attention more than a shout would. The coldness in her eyes made me shiver.

"Agreed," said George. "Come, Emily, let's confront her."

"No!" Adelaide grabbed his hand and he sat back on the seat, looking as dazed as if she'd slapped him. "She has asked for the afternoon off. I think you should wait and follow her when she leaves."

"You're right." George petted her hand. "A very clever suggestion."

"Mrs. White is not acting alone," Lady Preston said. She did not seem to notice that George and Adelaide were still touching. Her hard gaze locked with mine. "Follow her and find out who her accomplice is. Stop them before they can do more harm to my son."

"I will. I promise you, Lady Preston, I will not let them succeed." If only I felt as confident as I sounded.

She blinked rapidly and her gaze softened. "I know you will, Miss Chambers. You've been very good to us, and to my boy."

Lady Preston and Adelaide alighted from the coach and bid us farewell. George watched them go until they were out of sight.

Another hour passed before Mrs. White left number twelve Grosvenor Street. She walked to Oxford Street then hailed a passing omnibus that swerved out of the traffic to collect her. We followed in the carriage, stopping well back every time the omnibus let passengers off. It traveled through the suburbs at a fast clip and by the time Mrs. White finally stepped off, it was obvious she was heading to Leviticus Price's house.

"I'm sorry, George, but it does seem like he's involved after all."

"Perhaps," he said on a sigh, "but I still think Blunt is very much involved too." He got out of the carriage and offered his hand to assist me down the step.

"As do I."

We followed her to Price's house, but turned our backs when the door opened, so that we would not be seen.

"Now what?" George asked. "Should we knock first or simply burst in?"

"Unless you want to break down the door, I suggest we knock."

"Wait a moment." He returned to the carriage and reappeared a moment later, patting his hip.

"You've got a pistol under your jacket?"

"Of course. Do you want the other?"

"No, thank you. I'll leave the shooting to you. Let's hope it won't be necessary."

"I couldn't agree more."

We knocked on the front door. It was a long time before the landlady answered it and from her harried expression, she didn't look very pleased to have visitors. I quickly placed my foot inside so that she could not slam the door in our faces.

"What do you want?" she whispered, thrusting her prominent chin at us.

"Answers," George said.

"We are busy. Go away." She spoke with an accent. I'd noticed it before, but this time it seemed more pronounced, as if she'd been attempting to hide it previously but decided against the ruse now.

"We know what you're doing," George said.

"I am standing here waiting for you to leave. *That* is what I am doing."

I'd had enough. We had not come so far to walk away without answers and I refused to be intimidated. Besides, if we didn't get answers here and now, we'd be at a dead end.

George seemed to have the same idea. He pulled out his gun.

The landlady rubbed her hands down her apron and the nostrils in her sharp nose flared. She stepped back to let us in.

George insisted on going up first. I followed close behind, turning often to see what the landlady was doing. I didn't trust her, but she did not attempt anything untoward. At the top of the stairs, George pushed open the door to Price's parlor.

"They have a gun!" the landlady shouted before we could speak. "I could not stop them."

"Good lord," George murmured, taking in the scene in the small parlor.

I gasped and clapped a hand over my mouth as bile burned my throat. Mrs. White stood over the half-naked figure of Blunt, lying on the sofa, what appeared to be a brass syringe in her hand. It was poised to plunge into his bare arm.

"What are you doing?" I cried.

"I think I know," said George. He aimed the pistol at Mrs. White. "Don't move."

"No!" Blunt cried. He tried to sit up but fell back to the sofa. His face was pasty white and glistened with sweat. He was in the grip of opium withdrawal again.

"It's not what you think," Mrs. White said. Her hand trembled and the syringe was in danger of stabbing Blunt by accident.

"Put it down slowly," I said.

She pulled her hand back but did not let go of the syringe.

"What's in it? What are you injecting into him?"

"It's a...medicine," she said through lips stretched into a grim line. "To cure him."

Price sat on a chair near Blunt's head. His face was as gray as his long beard and he looked much older than the last time we'd seen him. The hands resting on the arms of the chair were paper thin and as wrinkled as dried prunes. He didn't speak but watched the proceedings with interest.

"Cure him?" George asked. "What do you mean?"

Mrs. White seemed to be the only one capable of speaking. Or the only one with answers. "We're going to cure him of his addiction," she said. "It's the latest treatment."

"Don't shoot her," Blunt pleaded. He tried to get up again but flopped back into the cushions once more. He breathed heavily, and his face suddenly distorted with pain. He gripped his stomach and moaned. I expected him to throw up at any moment into the bedpan placed on the floor beside him. As awful as the sight was, I didn't dare look away.

Mrs. White and Price exchanged unreadable glances. Then she pressed the syringe against Blunt's arm.

"Put it down!" I shouted, taking a step forward.

Her fingers tightened around the brass cylinder. Blunt squeezed his eyes shut. His lips turned whiter and his breaths came hard and fast, puffing out his cheeks.

She wasn't going to stop.

I was paralyzed, unsure if lunging at her would make the situation better or worse. In the end, it didn't matter.

George pulled the trigger.

Mrs. White screamed and dropped the syringe. Price lunged for it, but he was too slow and I reached it first.

Blunt clutched his leg and howled like an animal. The sickening sound clawed at my already shredded nerves.

"You shot him!" Mrs. White's shaking hands tore at Blunt's blood-stained trouser leg, ripping it to shreds.

"My sofa!" the landlady cried. "You will ruin it!"

Mrs. White worked quickly to staunch the blood flow. She shouted orders at the landlady to fetch clean cloths and bandages. Price merely sat there, watching. The long fingers of one hand slowly stroked his beard. The fingers of his other were wrapped around the chair arm, the knuckles stark against the dark wood grain. He did not look at us but at Blunt.

Beside me, George began to shake. "Will he, uh, be all right?" I gripped his arm, as much to steady myself as him. I wasn't sure which of us trembled more.

Mrs. White snatched the bandages from the landlady, giving her a glare that would have made me take a step back if I'd been the object of it. The landlady didn't move but stared at her, her eyes as fathomless as deep, cold lakes.

"Emily..." George whispered. "We should go."

"We can't go. We don't have answers yet." My grip tightened around his arm. We were so close. I would not let our fear and disgust drive us away empty-handed.

"Can I still have it?" Blunt pleaded with Mrs. White. "Please. Please, can I still have my...my medicine?" He was sobbing like a child denied a toy when all his friends were allowed to play with it.

"Not now," she said as she efficiently wound the bandage around his leg. "Not when you're in this state. You've lost too much blood. It would be too dangerous." She glanced at Price then at us. She wiped her brow with the back of her hand. "I'm sorry."

Tears streamed down Blunt's cheeks and spittle foamed at the corner of his mouth. "You've ruined everything," he snarled at us. "Everything!"

"Get out." Price's quiet voice cut through Blunt's wails like a sharp blade.

"What's in the syringe?" I pressed, ignoring him. "You were going to kill Blunt, weren't you?"

"I told you," Mrs. White said. "It was medicine to cure him. I can't give it to him when he's like this. Go. Go!"

"You had better do what he says," the landlady said to us. "Nothing more will happen here. Not now." She spoke with calm authority, and perhaps it was that which made me see her point more than hysterics could. No one was in any state to answer us and we had at least stopped them.

I took George's hand and dragged him out of the parlor. I wanted to smuggle out the syringe before anyone remembered it anyway. The landlady followed us downstairs and opened the door. George was still shaking and I gently removed the pistol from his grip as we crossed the threshold. The landlady slammed the door in our faces.

I stared at it for several moments, trying to take in everything that had just happened.

"I can't believe I did that." George looked down at his shaking hands. "Can't believe it."

"He'll be all right. You may have even saved him. Saved the entire Otherworld too. I'm not convinced Blunt was about to be cured of his addiction. I think Mrs. White was going to kill him so he could deliver the curse."

I instructed the driver to go to my house at speed. I put the dueling pistol back in its velvet bed inside the wooden case and took the syringe from the pocket in my skirt folds where I'd slipped it.

"Careful," George said. "Whatever is in that may have ended Blunt's life, albeit temporarily. Best if we don't touch it until we get out of the rocking coach."

I pocketed the syringe again and drew in a deep breath, the first proper one since entering Price's house. It didn't stop my nerves from jangling.

"Those people are despicable," spat George. "It seems they're all involved. The whole rotten lot of them."

I tipped my head back against the wall, dislodging my hat and a few hair pins. "I'm so saddened at Mrs. White's involvement. She seemed so nice. According to Lucy, Mrs. White was an inspiring teacher."

"Don't be disheartened. She must have been terribly upset over her son's death to go to such great lengths to hurt Beaufort."

"Revenge," I muttered. "It can do horrible things to good people."

"At least we thwarted their plans for a little while. We have their syringe and Blunt is in no condition to be...killed and brought back to life. By the looks of Price, he couldn't endure such an ordeal either."

"There is always the landlady and they could get another syringe. Oh, George, what shall we do now?"

George swapped seats and settled beside me. His presence was a comfort and I felt so glad to have him at my side. "At least we know who is involved now. Beaufort's killer can be brought to justice."

I shivered. "We must tell Lord and Lady Preston. Perhaps their investigators can work on Blunt and Mrs. White and find enough evidence to bring them to trial. But only *after* we reverse their curse on the Otherworld. If Lord Preston acts too soon, we're unlikely to get their co-operation."

"You think they'll co-operate now?"

"Perhaps. We need to find something to blackmail them

with. Something they want more than revenge on Jacob. And we must find it soon."

We thought about that for a moment, but neither of us had any suggestions. "I'm not sorry that Blunt is involved," George said. "He's a despicable character and deserves whatever he gets. Even the occasional bullet wound."

"Good lord, George, you're positively bloodthirsty."

He suddenly went quite pale and bent over double. His hat tumbled onto the floor and he did not pick it up. "Then why do I want to throw up?" he mumbled into his knees.

I removed my glove and pressed my hand to the back of his neck. He groaned but did not vomit, thank goodness. "Better?" I asked after a moment.

"Much. My apologies, Emily."

"No need to apologize. It was a rather gruesome sight."

"I hope they get him to a hospital soon," he said, straightening.

Blunt had indeed lost a lot of blood by the time we left, but Mrs. White had bound the wound tightly. He should be all right.

"What was Price's role in all this, do you think?" I asked.

He shrugged. "Difficult to say. He didn't seem to be participating in the proceedings at all."

"He looked quite ill, didn't he?"

George nodded, thoughtful. Neither of us spoke for the remainder of the journey.

***

When we finally arrived at my house, Lucy had luncheon waiting for us. George and I gave Celia and Cara the edited version of the morning's events. There was no reason to alarm either of them when they could do nothing about it. Celia in particular would be unbearable if she knew a pistol had been fired.

"So it has come to an end?" She eyed me closely, her boiled eggs forgotten. It would seem she didn't quite believe we had found our villain.

"Almost," I said. "We'll report what we know to Lord

Preston, but not until after we stop them destroying the Otherworld. As to how we will do that..." I shrugged.

She seemed satisfied with that answer and continued eating. George and Cara ate heartily too, but I merely picked at my eggs and bacon.

"Oh, I almost forgot," Celia said. "We picked up your gown this morning."

"It's beautiful," Cara gushed. "All that satin and lace...I wish I could have a gown like that."

"One day you will," I said. "There will be balls aplenty for you when you're older."

"You sound positively parental, Emily," George teased.

"Indeed she does." Celia smiled at me. "She's grown up so fast. Soon she shall be married and have children of her own." She sniffed.

"Good lord, Celia, stop marrying me off."

"No, I won't stop. It's my greatest wish to see you settled. Besides, it may not be as far away as all that. Mr. Hyde is quite taken with you. It's obvious in the way he looks at you."

I blushed fiercely and concentrated on my plate to hide my embarrassment.

Cara made a miffed sound through her nose and set her fork down on her plate with a loud *clank*. When I raised my eyebrows at her she said, "Celia hasn't seen the way Mr. Beaufort looks at you, but I have."

"Enough," Celia said sharply. "Cara, are you finished? If so, you're free to the leave the table. Emily, I suggest you try on your gown in case there are any last minute alterations. It's too late to take it back to the dressmaker, but I can probably manage. Mr. Culvert, will you excuse us?"

"Of course. I'll wait in the drawing room. I need to sit quietly and think anyway."

I had just finished trying on my dress and was making my way into the drawing room to see George when a fierce pounding threatened to knock down the front door. Since Lucy was helping Celia adjust my gown in the small parlor

122

out the back, I opened it. Price's landlady stood there, her broad brimmed hat pulled low over her eyes. She glanced nervously over her shoulder.

"Shut the door," she said, pushing past me. "I don't think I was followed, but it is best to be cautious."

"Uh...what are you doing here?"

"Helping you."

"Helping us? How?"

"Is there somewhere we can sit and talk?"

I led her into the drawing room and George rose out of the armchair. "Good lord!" he said upon seeing her.

"We haven't been formally introduced," I said. "I am Emily Chambers and this is Mr. Culvert."

"Mrs. Stanley," she said, looking at her surroundings rather than at us. Our house was a little larger than her own, but our furniture just as old and worn, except for our new sofa, of course.

"So how can you help us?"

"First of all, you must know that Mr. Price is innocent, as am I."

"I think you'd better explain everything to us," George said. "Starting from the beginning."

"Very well." She sat on the edge of the chair and crossed her feet at the ankles, her reticule in her lap. She had not removed her hat or gloves and looked poised to run off at any moment like a skittish cat. "That *woman* and Blunt want to destroy the Otherworld. I *hate* her. She is the devil. Pure evil. You have delayed them, thank God."

George held up his hand for silence. "How about the *very* beginning, Mrs. Stanley?"

She drew a breath and let it out slowly. "That Mrs. White is behind it all. Her real name is Seymour. Her son killed himself and she blames your spirit friend for his death."

"Which is absurd," I said. "It had nothing to do with Jacob."

She shrugged. "Blunt is in love with her and she knows it. She is pulling his strings like a puppeteer. She made him get as much information about Otherworld matters from Mr. Price that he could and pass it along to her."

"So it was they who released the demon and were behind the summoning of Mortlock?" I asked.

She lifted that strong witchy chin and pointed it at me. "Yes. And now they are cursing the Otherworld, trying to destroy it and your friend in particular."

"With a curse they got from Mr. Price. I see, but how did *he* come to know of the curse? Indeed, any of the curses?"

"Through me. My kind are the keepers of many supernatural secrets that your kind know nothing about."

"You're Romany!"

"Fascinating," George said, pushing his glasses up his nose and peering closer.

"But your name does not sound Romany," I said.

"Stanley is the adopted name of my late husband's family. We use it when we travel in your world." Another proud tilt of her chin. Now that I knew her heritage, I could see the dark eyes of the gypsy and although her hair was mostly gray, it could have been black in her youth.

"So Mrs. White, or rather Mrs. Seymour, killed Jacob Beaufort?" I asked. "Are you prepared to swear to that in court?"

"Court is not for the likes of us, not when we are treated little better than animals in this country. I have told you what I know. It is up to you to bring that *curvă* and her *curist* to justice." From the way she spat out the Romany words, I got the feeling they weren't complimentary. "I am glad you came to my house today," she went on. "I have been worried about him."

"About Price?" George asked. "Have they been threatening him?"

"They have been killing him!"

"You mean he was the one who delivered the curse to the Otherworld?"

"That explains why he looked so ill," said George.

Mrs. Stanley pressed her gloved fingers to her nose. Her

eyes filled with tears. "I had the devil of a time trying to convince them he was not well enough to do it again. That is when Blunt decided to deliver the curse himself. There was no one else. I would not do it. They threatened me, tried to give me money, but I refused."

"That's very brave of you."

She glanced back to the door, then up at the ceiling, and finally at each of us. Her dark stare was bold, direct. "Not brave. I fear destroying the Otherworld more than I fear them. They may not care what happens to their souls after death, but I do. We Romany respect death and the spirit world. To destroy it is to destroy the life you will have beyond this one."

"Yes, I see." It made sense. I knew little about the gypsy culture, but if they were the guardians of such powerful paranormal curses, then it was logical that they would respect the supernatural. "Is that why you've come to us?"

"Yes. I do not want to be next to die. I do not want to be forced to help them. You have delayed the Otherworld's destruction, Miss Chambers, but not stopped it. You must deliver the counter curse before she finds another victim. The next time will be the third time the curse will be delivered."

"The third and final time," I murmured.

"Yes. This curse requires the power of three to work. How does it fare up there?"

"The Waiting Area is all but destroyed. Many spirits have been lost, the rest are fading away. I fear you're right, Mrs. Stanley. One more time will see the complete destruction of the Waiting Area and...and Jacob." I swallowed a sob. Now was not the time for hysterics or even melancholy. I needed to be strong and have my wits about me.

Mrs. Stanley pressed her hand over her mouth and uttered something in Romany. "That is very shocking to hear."

"We must have Mrs. White—Mrs. Seymour—arrested before she can find another victim to deliver the curse," I said. "She could easily pay a street urchin to do it."

"The curse is complicated, the language ancient and difficult for a non-Romany, particularly for an illiterate child. She tried a street boy once, but he could not get it right and died in the attempt."

"Oh my god! The poor boy."

"Terrible." George shook his head. "So what do you think she'll do next?"

"She will find someone else," Mrs. Stanley said. "A healthy adult who can be trained to speak the Romany words."

George lifted an eyebrow at me. "That could take time."

"That's not something I want to wager on," I said.

"Then we'll send the police to the Grosvenor Street house to arrest her for the murder of Beaufort."

"Not yet," Mrs. Stanley said quickly. "First she must send Miss Chambers to the Otherworld to deliver the counter curse."

"I say! I don't think Emily should do it."

Yet I had to. I knew it. Besides, I wanted to see what the Otherworld was like for myself. My entire life, I'd heard about it, thought about it, and curiosity had gnawed at me. "I'll do it," I said.

Mrs. Stanley nodded. "I think it is for the best. You are part of that world already with your special gift. Your presence there will be powerful, and that can only help."

"I don't like it," George hedged.

"You don't have to like it," I said. "I'm doing it regardless. But I don't trust Mrs. White. If what Mrs. Stanley says is true—"

"It is," she said with a flare of her nostrils.

"*If* what Mrs. Stanley says is true," I said again, "then Mrs. White cannot be trusted to bring me back. We could go to a hospital and ask them to..." *Kill me.*

"I do not think a doctor will put you to your death."

"She's right," George said. "Don't worry, Em, we'll all be there. Your sister too, if you want her. We will force Mrs.

White to keep you alive."

I sat for a moment, not yet believing what I'd agreed to do. Could I trust Mrs. Stanley? I felt a little mad for going along with her scheme. Actually, more than a little, particularly since I was rather looking forward to it. To see the Otherworld, to see Jacob again...I couldn't deny that it sent a little thrill through me.

"Until we are ready, Mrs. Seymour should be left alone," Mrs. Stanley said. "If we startle her, she will leave London and we will face delays as we try to find another to perform the death and resurrection."

"Agreed," George said.

"Mrs. Stanley," I asked, "where is your tribe?"

"My people will be south of Codicote in Hertfordshire at this time of year. Why?"

"Because you don't have the counter curse, do you? You must not, otherwise you would have had Price deliver it on his last visit to the Otherworld. He could have tricked Mrs. White and delivered the counter curse instead of the one she gave him."

She pressed her hand to her nose once more and I expected to see tears pool, but none did. Her eyes were two black orbs that held my gaze steadily. "Of course I do not have it."

"How long will it take you to reach your people's camp?" I asked.

"I can leave today and be back late tomorrow."

"Only if you rode very fast. I can lend you my carriage," George said.

"Mr. Culvert, my people are excellent horsemen and women. We can ride bareback at speed for twenty days and twenty nights if necessary."

"I'll take that as your refusal of my offer," he muttered.

"Late tomorrow," I said. "That will have to be soon enough."

"We have the ball tomorrow night," George said. "You cannot miss that, Em. It's the event of the century!"

"This is more important. Mrs. Stanley, if you haven't arrived here by the time I must leave for the ball, come fetch me at Lord and Lady Preston's Belgrave Square house upon your return. We'll go to Mrs. White's place of work together and force her to inject me. We'll trick her into thinking I'll be delivering the curse."

"Trick her how?" George asked. "She's no fool."

"I will tell her that you are going to deliver the curse," Mrs. Stanley said. "She doesn't know I have told you everything and will believe me. I will tell her that *you* think you are delivering the counter curse and that is why you have agreed to do it, otherwise she will be suspicious."

I nodded. So did George, reluctantly. "I still don't like it," he said.

Mrs. Stanley was eager to get on her way to fetch the counter curse from her people and did not stay for tea as politeness dictated.

"Should we trust her?" George asked after she'd left.

It was the same question I'd been asking myself ever since she walked in. "We don't have a choice."

"Yes, we do." He pushed his glasses up his nose and gave me a somewhat smug smile. "I can go independently to her tribe. If she shows up, then we know she's telling the truth. If she doesn't—"

"Then we'll know she lied and never intended to get the counter curse." I didn't tell him that by the time he discovered which side Mrs. Stanley's loyalties lay, it might be too late.

CHAPTER 10

"Don't go alone," I said to George. "Take Theo and Louis."

"Your father?"

"He's a brave man and looks strong. You may need him."

"I'm beginning to think you doubt my abilities when it comes to taking care of myself."

"George." I squared up to him. "You are a gentle man, and you are about to confront a clan of gypsies. I do not think even the three of you will be quite safe, but there's nothing for it but to go."

"You may be right." He removed his coat from the hook near the front door and brushed the sleeve with a flick of his fingers.

I pecked him on the cheek. "Good luck, and be careful."

"Don't worry. I'll have my pistols."

I didn't tell him that two pistols would hardly protect him from a clan of gypsies if they decided they didn't like him. "Just a thought, but it may be better to let my father do the talking. Your manner can be somewhat aloof at times and Theo doesn't seem to like them at all."

He tugged the brim of his hat down. "Emily, you worry too much. Trust me. I know how to handle a group of ruffians."

Oh dear. If my father didn't take charge, the task was doomed.

George left and I quickly grew restless. There was little to do at home except watch Celia adjust the hem on my gown and play cards with Cara. It rained briefly, but once it cleared I decided to walk to Grosvenor Street and see if Mrs. White was still at number twelve.

The brisk stroll in the cool air worked wonders on my frustration and I arrived at Grosvenor Square very quickly. I watched number twelve for a short time but there was no sign of Mrs. White. Since the sky threatened rain once more, it was doubtful if she would take her charges out—if she did indeed still work there—so I decided to visit her instead.

Well, not *her* exactly. I questioned a maid leaving via the servants' stairs. She said Mrs. White had suddenly resigned her position as governess that afternoon, leaving the mistress a note and not even saying goodbye to her charges or the other staff. Apparently everyone in the household was shocked by her decision.

I was not. Mrs. White must be worried that we would send the police to her door or, worse, Lord Preston. Hopefully Mrs. Stanley knew where to find her or our plan would come to naught. We needed Mrs. White to think I was delivering the curse so that she would not try to find anyone else in the meantime.

It began to rain so I huddled under my umbrella as I headed back to Druids Way. Lucy had a welcoming cup of warm chocolate waiting for me. I sipped it in the cozy private parlor as Celia worked on the hem of my gown and Cara dozed by the fireplace. It was terribly difficult not to wonder how George, Theo, and Louis fared as night fell. How far had they traveled? Where would they stay overnight? Was my father a good horseman and what did he think of their strange task? I didn't like thinking of the three of them confronting an unpredictable gypsy tribe, but it was better to do that than let my mind wonder to Jacob.

I felt sick to my stomach whenever I recalled how he

looked the last few times I'd seen him. It was like watching a pair of butterfly wings slowly disintegrate in the sun. Soon he would be nothing. Not even a spirit. My heart clenched like a fist and punched into my ribs. I may never see him again, neither in this realm nor in the Otherworld. If Mrs. White succeeded, we would never be together.

Eternity without the man I loved was a bleak and miserable prospect.

I set down my chocolate cup because my shaking hands could no longer hold it steady.

"At least we have something pleasant to look forward to," Celia said, studying her handiwork.

I stared at her, trying to think through the mire of dark thoughts clogging my mind. But I could not. All I wanted to do was curl up into a ball and make Jacob better through sheer willpower.

When I didn't answer, Celia looked up. She frowned but said nothing. "All this business with the spirits, Louis' return, and now the cancelations...we deserve an enjoyable evening."

"Yes, of course," I said, not really listening.

"How many dances has Theo reserved with you?"

"How many...? You mean the ball?" I shrugged. "I don't recall. None, I think."

Celia dropped her hands to her lap and regarded me. "What do you mean? He must have reserved some dances. He's very taken with you. It's as clear as the nose on my face."

I rubbed my forehead. "Perhaps he has. I don't remember."

"Emily." I could tell from the tone of her voice that I was about to receive a lecture. Ordinarily I would make excuses and leave, but I no longer cared. Let her say whatever was on her mind. What did it matter anymore? "Emily, do not let him think you are in love with another."

"I'm not. I mean, I'm not giving him that impression." At least, I didn't think so. I sighed. "I'm sure we'll dance together tomorrow night."

"You *are* looking forward to the ball, are you not?"

"Of course. I just wish there were not so many other burdens to be endured. It colors the experience somewhat."

"I know, Em, I know. But you *will* resolve this as you've resolved the other situations. I have the utmost faith in you, my girl." Her quiet, determined voice compelled me to look at her. Tears shone in her eyes but she was smiling a little. It was not a smile I could decipher. "Emily, if he declares himself at the ball, what will you say?"

"Declares himself! Oh...I...do you think he will?"

"I think it likely. Please, do not throw away this opportunity. Emily...being settled to a good man is not an easy thing to achieve. There are not too many to be had, unfortunately." She looked down at her fingers, still clutching the needle and the hem of my gown. "Take my situation, for example. I had three men court me. If I'd known then what I know now, I would have accepted one."

"Do not think like that, Celia. They were good men, but you didn't love any of them. Mama knew it, as did I." I moved to sit beside her and covered her hand with my own. She did not look up but her lashes were damp even though her cheeks were dry. "Celia, a lifetime is a long time to be with someone you don't love."

"Oh, Emily." She heaved a deep sigh. "I commend you for your idealism. I really do. But making decisions based on your heart's desire can lead to disaster. In Mama's case, it did not, but in mine...in mine..." She sniffed and closed her eyes. I squeezed her hands harder. "In mine, waiting for love has led me to long years of loneliness. I should not have waited. I would have been perfectly happy with one of those other men. Good, solid men with good, solid work. They're all married now, and they're all happy."

I withdrew my hands. "And you are not."

She looked up sharply. Her eyes were large pools. "Oh, Em! No, I didn't mean that. I am very happy with you. And with Cara. I adore you, you know that."

"But you are not fulfilled. Something is missing." Until

I'd said it, I didn't realize how much I understood my sister. She *did* love me. I knew that without a doubt. But one day I would move on. As would Cara. Celia craved something that was just hers alone, forever. A husband to cherish always, children, a home that had *her* stamp on it, not Mama's.

"Do not wait, Emily. Do not throw your future away over a man who can never be there. This love you feel for him...it will fade over time."

I shook my head and was about to protest, but she put a finger to my lips, shushing me.

"It will always be within you, like a dull ache, but the intensity will dampen and other loves will make up for its loss. Children, a husband who adores you. And Theo does love you. Any fool can see it. Please...love him back or at least accept him and care for him. For your sake. And for Jacob's."

"Jacob?" I swallowed but couldn't dislodge the lump in my throat.

"If he loves you, he will want you to have a full life. He would not wish you to be unhappy, not even for a moment, let alone decades."

Tears slid down my cheeks and dripped off my chin onto my lap. "He does want my happiness." I was shaking, my body quivering like a jelly. "He said...he said Theo would be good to me."

She put her arm around my shoulders and pulled me to her. Our foreheads touched and although I couldn't see her face, I knew she was crying too. "Then you must marry Theo Hyde. Live long with him at your side, love him and be loved in return. You deserve nothing less."

My heart cracked and I turned into her shoulder. Great, heaving sobs wracked me and I felt like I was being turned inside out, my soul exposed. I had always prided myself on being emotionally strong, but at that moment, I felt as weak as a little child. It was a long time before I could speak and when I did, my voice did not sound like my own. "I do want to give up being a medium, performing at soirees and afternoon teas. I'm tired of it, Celia. I suppose Theo could give me a life where I don't have to do it anymore."

"Emily...I did not know the extent of your dislike for your work." She wiped away my tears with her thumbs. "I'm sorry, I—"

"Don't apologize. I know we needed the money and I wanted to help our situation. But if I were to wed Theo..." The idea of marrying him was still so new to me, I could not yet put it into words.

"A lawyer would make a good wage," she finished for me. "It won't be necessary for you to work once you are wed." She smiled through her tears. "Just as well because all of our séances have been canceled."

"All! Surely not everyone has heard about our last two failures. And if they have, I'm surprised they think that's reason enough to cancel."

"It's not just the difficulty summoning spirits. It's worse." She tucked a strand of my hair behind my ear. "Some are saying you are a fraud, true, but others claim you release evil spirits." She waved a hand in dismissal. "Ridiculous claims and I told them so."

I slumped back into the sofa. Celia, quite recovered, told me to sit up straight like a young lady. "So you see, you must secure Theo Hyde soon," she said. "Tomorrow night. At the ball." She nodded at Cara who still slept, or feigned sleep, by the fireplace. "Our future depends on it."

***

I lay awake in the darkness of my bedroom thinking about a life with Theo. Would I like to marry him? Could I do it? Every time I closed my eyes and thought about our wedding day and beyond, the face that came to me wasn't Theo's but Jacob's. And when I thought about Jacob, and what lay ahead for him, I couldn't stop crying. I sobbed into the pillow until there was no breath left in me and I could only make little gasping noises.

"Don't be sad."

I was so drained that I couldn't even twitch in surprise at

the sound of Jacob's voice. I rolled over and could just make out his fuzzy outline in the darkness. With his superior spirit sight, he could probably see my puffy eyes and red nose. I didn't care.

"Jacob." I sat up. "Are you all right? Should you be here? Doesn't it make you weaker?"

He sat on the edge of my bed near my hip. The mattress hardly depressed, so light was he. "You know I can't stay away from you, no matter what."

"But—"

"Shhh." He leaned down and kissed my damp cheek. "Don't worry about it. Tell me why you're so upset."

"I...it's nothing. Forget about me. Jacob, something important has happened. We discovered that Mrs. White is the one who killed you. She's behind the curses. George, Theo, and Louis are fetching a counter curse as we speak." I caressed his cheek with the back of my hand. "It'll all be resolved very soon. Everything will return to normal in the Waiting Area and you...you will be able to crossover. We have your killer."

He sighed and his body seemed to relax a little. "Thank God," he murmured. "Emily, you are a marvel."

"It was you who set us on the trail of Mrs. White. If you hadn't discovered she was Frederick Seymour's mother, we would still be in the dark." I cupped his face in my hands. It was cold.

"I cannot tell you how relieved I am to hear you speak of this being over. So many spirits have gone. The Administrators too. There is only me and a handful of others holding on up there. It's so difficult, Em. It takes so much out of me."

"Then you must go. Go back there and rest. Do not spend all your energy here." I gave his shoulder a gentle shove, but he did not leave.

He took my hands and pressed them to his lips. "Emily...I needed..." He disappeared and I held my breath, but thankfully he returned in the same position. "...need to see you...last time."

"This is not the last time." I rose up on my knees on the bed and clutched his shirt, twisting the linen in my fists. "Jacob, it will soon be over. You must hang on until tomorrow night."

"...try." He smiled sadly. "If all...well...crossover anyway. So this...bye."

"No! No, it's not goodbye." I shook my fists, still holding onto his shirt. Hot tears burned my cheeks again and it felt like they would never end. "I'm not ready. Not yet. Jacob..."

He gently pried my fingers out of his shirt then drew me to him and wrapped his arms around me like a blanket. I cried into his chest until there was nothing left but deep, aching sorrow.

We stayed like that, with my head tucked beneath his chin and his arms around me, for a long time. It wasn't until he began to shiver that I pulled away.

"You're cold," I said.

"A little."

"Let me warm you."

"I don't think...can."

"How do you know? Has anyone else tried?"

"Jealous?" He sounded amused.

"Come lie with me." I lifted the edge of the bedcovers.

"...shouldn't."

"I don't care about what we should and should not do. Jacob, this may be the last time we see each other. Can you not forget propriety for a few moments and lie with me?"

I took his hand and guided him down. He rested his head on the pillow beside mine and stretched out his long legs beneath the covers. I linked my fingers with his between us.

"Promise...not to...advantage of me?" he said with a smile in his voice.

I laughed. "I'll try, although I am sorely tempted."

"So am I," he whispered.

I leaned closer and found his mouth with my own. Our light, teasing kisses were like tiny sparks upon impact, then something within me ignited and I deepened the kiss. Warmth spread down my spine, between my thighs, all the way to my toes, and I hoped he felt it too. He groaned, a loud sound compared to the whispered words he'd been speaking. Then he broke the kiss but did not pull away.

"Emily," he murmured against my lips. "Ah, Em... wish...lie...forever."

"We will," I heard myself say. "One day. We will be together."

"Promise...promise me...don't give up...on life." He lifted himself up on one elbow and regarded me from above. I wished it weren't so dark so I could see him, but perhaps it was for the best that I couldn't. The fierce intensity with which he spoke alarmed me enough. "Don't...for me."

"I promise to live a full life here," I said with as much conviction as my aching heart could muster. "But I cannot promise I will be happy." I opened my arms and he lowered himself into them. "Satisfied?"

His answer was a deep, shuddering sigh. We held each other, chest to chest and hip to hip, and there we stayed as he grew weaker toward dawn. Finally, as I lay in that foggy place between awake and sleep, he faded away completely.

***

The Beaufort house in Belgrave Square was like a beacon in the clear spring night. Light blazed from all the windows and the lamps on the guests' coaches formed a bright, swaying river along the street. Celia and I had intended to hire a hansom to take us but one of George's carriages arrived unannounced, minus George of course. He'd thought of everything.

We were delivered to the ball in grand style, made even grander by my gown. It was fit for a princess. Of the palest gold, it was decorated with ruffles of lace on the skirt and across the neckline, with an elegant bustle cascading to the floor at the back. A cluster of pink rosettes on each small sleeve at the shoulders matched the ones in my hair. No one who saw me would think me out of place at Adelaide

Beaufort's ball.

It was difficult to appreciate the moment, however. The memory of Jacob's body lying next to me, cold and weak, was still so strong and dampened my enthusiasm. Mrs. Stanley had not come to me with the counter curse, nor had George.

We left our shawls with the maid in the ladies' dressing room and joined the procession to greet Adelaide and her parents.

"Where's Mr. Culvert?" Adelaide whispered, after complimenting me on my gown.

"Delayed," I said. "He really wants to be here, but there was an urgent errand he had to make first."

Her smile slipped. "Oh. I do hope he won't be long. I've reserved two dances for him but if he doesn't show soon, I'll have to cross his name off my card."

"Keep the dances open," I said. "He would be extremely disappointed to miss out."

Her cheeks reddened. "Would he? Oh, good. I mean, not good that he'd be disappointed, just good that he wishes to dance with me."

"Come along, Emily," Celia said. "You're holding everyone up."

"You look extraordinarily pretty tonight," Adelaide said as I moved toward her mother. "I'm sure your dance card will fill quickly."

I wasn't in the mood to dance, but I smiled anyway. "And you look lovely," I told her. She did indeed. The pink gown set off her creamy complexion and she seemed to glow from within. I hoped her night would not be ruined.

From the reception I received from Lord Preston, standing beside his wife, I wasn't so sure the night would go off without a hitch. I got the distinct impression he didn't want me there. I curtseyed to him as was required, but he barely acknowledged my presence, or Celia's. We both moved into the ballroom as quickly as possible.

"Odious man," my sister muttered. She stopped short at

the entrance to the grand ballroom. "Oh my. Emily, look at all these people!"

Hundreds of men and women dressed in beautiful gowns and suits amassed around the edges of the room. Beyond them, I caught glimpses of dancers swirling to the music. Laughter and chatter created its own throbbing beat that pulsed through my limbs, my temples. The room itself seemed like a living, breathing thing, and I suddenly felt like a small creature in its path, a morsel to be devoured. I did not belong there. These fine people were not part of my world, nor I theirs.

I edged closer to Celia, but she didn't seem to notice my sudden timidity. "All these gentlemen," she said, tugging the rosette on my sleeve down another inch. My shoulders were already bared, but she seemed to think that not enough. "There, better."

"Celia, we don't know any gentlemen here," I protested. "It's all for no use." A lady and gentleman could not introduce themselves, not even at a ball. They had to wait until a mutual acquaintance performed the introduction. The only people we knew there were Adelaide and her parents and they were busy greeting guests.

"We shall have to wait for Lady Preston," Celia said. "In the meantime, I see no reason for you to go unnoticed."

I saw every reason to go unnoticed among all those people. All those *normal*, high society people.

We moved further into the room, the guests parting for us like a warm knife slicing through butter. Then the whispers began. Some turned away as I passed but others stared openly. One or two pointed.

"...a fraud," said a plump woman.

"An odd creature," said her friend.

"No *lady* has hair like that."

"Lady Preston must have lost her mind..." said another.

"...cannot summon a sneeze let alone a spirit." That comment elicited a series of tinkling laughs from the listeners.

"...malicious ghosts..."

"Evil follows her."

"Are you surprised? Her kind are bad luck."

Celia's arm tightened on mine as she steered me through the crowd. I felt their words as sharply as an elbow to the ribs or a blow to the head. Indeed, I suddenly felt as though I had been struck. The lights in the chandeliers above blurred, the room swum, and the overwhelming scent of perfume made me dizzy.

"Air," I gasped. "Celia..." My knees buckled and I swooned.

"Here, Miss Chambers, follow me." A man took firm hold of my other arm and I was half-marched, half-carried between he and Celia into another room. They settled me on a chair in the corner and I realized I was in the refreshment room. Being early, it was mercifully empty except for a handful of unfortunate girls who felt as uncomfortable in the ballroom as I did. Yet even they turned their backs and began whispering to each other behind their hands. I suppose it is always a happy event to see someone less fortunate that yourself.

"Emily, are you all right?" asked Celia, sitting beside me. She held my hand so hard it was beginning to tingle.

I nodded and squinted at the back of my rescuer as he stood at the refreshment table. He was large with thinning blond hair. I recognized him immediately.

"Thank you, Mr. Arbuthnot," I said when he approached with two glasses of lemonade. I accepted one and Celia took the other.

"That was very kind of you to help us," she said. "Emily isn't used to balls, you see. Perhaps the lights, the people..." Her excuses were unnecessary. We all knew the real reason for my shock. I hated being the center of attention, but to have so many people staring and talking about me at once was like drowning in mud. I felt the weight of their opinions pressing down on me, suffocating.

"Do you feel better, Miss Chambers?" he asked, all

politeness. He didn't mention the whispers and stares. He was a true gentleman.

"Much better. Thank you." I felt a little sheepish. I'd forgotten he would be at the ball. I hadn't seen Theo's cousin for two weeks, not since the spirit of Mortlock had possessed him then exited his body to enter George's. We'd never told Wallace Arbuthnot what had happened, but I'd often wondered if he remembered any of it, or if he guessed. George had eventually recalled some events and I thought Wallace might too, but then George was aware of the supernatural whereas Wallace was still in the dark. Or so we assumed.

"You look better already," he said, cheerfully. "I would offer to dance with you, but I've two left feet. I'm afraid dancing with me is a fate most young ladies wish to avoid."

The door to the balcony opened and a young woman in an exquisite pale blue dress entered the refreshment room. She checked her red curls were still pinned securely and adjusted the gown at her breast so that it didn't reveal quite so much of her luscious figure. With her head dipped, she hurried past us and out of the room, but not before I saw her secretive smile. Celia clicked her tongue and Wallace pretended he hadn't noticed, but I was glad someone was enjoying themselves with their lover on the balcony. Perhaps I could escape out there later.

"It's a shame you don't dance, Mr. Arbuthnot," Celia said, picking up the thread of our conversation. "However, it may be best if Emily avoided the activity altogether too. Perhaps you could introduce her to some of your friends instead. We know so few people here, you see."

I wanted to kick her. Her blatant bad manners were so unlike her, although I suppose it was a testament to her desperation. No doubt she would prefer Theo be the one to rescue me, but since he wasn't there, she probably thought she should find me a substitute marital prospect. I sighed and wished Mrs. Stanley would interrupt my misery.

"I would be delighted to introduce you to my friends,"

Wallace said, with no false enthusiasm that I could detect. "But you know more people here than you think, Miss Chambers. My cousin, Theodore Hyde, is around somewhere."

"Theo?" I shook my head. "No, he's with George Culvert. They had an, uh, urgent errand to run."

Wallace's chins wobbled as he shook his head. "You're mistaken, Miss Chambers. Theo is definitely here. We came together. He wouldn't miss an occasion like this for the world."

Theo was at the ball? The evening suddenly didn't seem so awful.

"Ah, there he...oh." Wallace cleared his throat and moved to block my view.

But I'd already seen Theo, and seen the direction from which he'd come—the door leading out to the balcony. The same door through which the redheaded girl had entered moments before. It was clear to anyone who saw her that she'd had an assignation with a lover and came in ahead of him to throw off suspicion.

That lover was Theo.

CHAPTER 11

Celia gasped loudly and Theo stopped dead. His eyes widened when he saw us and I could see the moment when he realized we knew what he'd been doing out on the balcony. He seemed to be caught between approaching us and running away.

I opened my mouth to say something, but nothing came out. I was much too stunned to form coherent sentences.

Celia gripped my hand and set down her glass on the table beside her. She said nothing, but I could feel the anger simmering inside her through our linked hands.

Wallace's cough shattered the uneasy silence. "I, uh, have to go and..." He bowed to us then scuttled out of the refreshment room.

To my great surprise, Theo didn't follow him. I commended him for his bravery. I would not want to face Celia at such a moment if I were in his shoes.

"May we have a few minutes?" he asked her.

Celia's grip tightened. "You dare to—"

"Celia," I said sharply. "I'd like to speak to Theo. Alone."

I thought she wouldn't leave, but finally she rose. With a savage glare that was lost on Theo because he wasn't looking at her but at me, she strode to the refreshment table, out of earshot. I lifted both my eyebrows at her and she turned her back and stood as rigid as a pole.

"Well," I said. "This is rather awkward."

"Emily..." Theo drew in a breath. "Hell."

"It is, isn't it? Perhaps you should sit down. I find that helps when I'm feeling nauseous."

He sat in the seat Celia had vacated, eyeing me carefully as if I were a bubble about to burst in his face. "Emily, I'm so sorry." At least he had the decency not to proclaim his innocence.

"Don't be. I'm not. Stunned, yes, but not sorry."

He blinked rapidly. "Why not? Why aren't you angry with me? I deserve it. God, how I deserve it."

"How can I be sorry when I don't love you?"

"You don't?" He frowned. "But I thought...I thought we had something special. I thought...that you loved me. I certainly loved you."

The absurdity made me laugh. Celia glanced over her shoulder at us. "Theo, how can you love me considering...?" I waved my hand at the door leading out to the balcony. "...considering that?"

"What Suzette and I share is not love, Emily. That is...self-preservation."

"You're not making much sense."

He splayed his fingers across his knees and studied them intently. "It comes down to the fact that I don't want to be a lawyer."

"I see. Actually, no I don't. How does your career have anything to do with me and her, Suzette?"

"I don't want to be a lawyer, a banker, or any other occupation acceptable to a gentleman of no means."

"Then what do you want to be?"

"A country gentleman. Emily." He met my gaze and I was struck by the raw emotions in his eyes. I hadn't expected that. I'd expected lies and false flattery, but the rawness chipped away at the wall I'd begun to build around myself the moment I saw him enter from the balcony. "I want to return to Shropshire and my home. My land. I want to nurture it back to the way it used to be before my father let it fall into ruin. I want to farm the fields again and live off the income. The estate could be profitable if some capital were invested in it. I love that parcel of land. If you could see it at this time of year, you would love it to."

"So you need to marry a woman with money to invest."

He nodded. "The banks would not give Father a loan, and unfortunately..." He spread his fingers again. "Unfortunately your business isn't all that profitable right now."

"That is quite the understatement," I muttered. "Even if it were, I doubt it would be enough for your needs."

He shook his head sadly. "Suzette is an heiress to a considerable fortune. I met her recently and I will ask her to marry me once I've secured her affections. I was going to tell you tonight, but it seems I should have done it earlier."

"I'll admit I would have preferred it. Celia too. I think she's going to be more upset about this than I am."

"Oh, Emily." He got down on his knees before me. "I adore you. I will always have a place in my heart for you." He reached for my hand but I withdrew it. I wasn't going to fall for any more of his lies, if indeed that's what they were. He sat back on the chair, his movements awkward and unsure.

"Do you love her, Theo? A lifetime is a long time to be with someone you do not love." It was the same thing I'd said to Celia earlier, but it was just as applicable.

"I like her very much. As to love..." He shrugged. "That may come, if she'll have me."

"Does she know you have no money?"

He nodded. "I don't want to trick her."

"Isn't pretending you love her a form of trickery?"

"What marriage is based on love anyway? Who can afford it except the very rich?"

He had me there. "Promise me something, Theo."

"Anything." He leaned closer.

"Be good to her for the rest of your lives together. Use her money wisely. Do not make her regret marrying you. Do not make her ashamed to be your wife."

He sucked in his lower lip and nodded once. He turned away and I waited as he composed himself. Finally, he looked at me again. "I've been imagining this moment for a few days. Dreading it. I admit that I expected some hysteria and name-calling. This reasonable response is quite unexpected and undeserved."

"Disappointed?"

"A little." He gave me a wry smile. "You don't seem at all upset. Indeed, you seem to be more concerned for Suzette than for yourself. You truly don't love me, do you?"

"I don't," I said quietly. "I care for you, but as to love..." I shook my head.

"You love another? Beaufort?"

I inclined my head as tears welled. "It's not an ideal match."

He spluttered a watery laugh. Through my blurry vision, I could just make out the shine in his eyes. "Well. I'm not entitled to claim an injury here, but I admit I feel wounded. I thought I loved you." He wiped away an errant tear before it reached his cheek. "I still do."

"You're right. You cannot claim an injury. You do not love me, Theo. You cannot." I held my hand up as he began to protest. "A man who truly loves a woman would do everything in his power to be with her. He would want to marry her despite poverty."

He barked a bitter, harsh laugh and I thought he would storm off, offended. He did not. "Perhaps you're right. I don't know. Instead of debating our feelings, let's promise to part as friends."

We shook hands, but he did not let mine go when I tried to leave. "Goodbye, Emily Chambers." He kissed my knuckles. "And good luck."

I watched him walk away. He bowed to my sister and she nodded back, her face so dark I thought she might scold him right there. But she let him go and returned to me.

"Are you all right?" she asked.

"Yes," I said on a sigh. "I'd be much better if I could leave."

"Then we shall."

I blinked at her. "But don't you want me to stay to meet a gentleman? Now that Theo is not available—"

"Emily." She faced me and gripped both my shoulders. "My dearest, you need time to overcome this disappointment."

"I am not all that disappointed. Truly. But I don't want to be sifting through marriageable gentleman right now either." I couldn't imagine I ever would, but I didn't tell my sister that.

She patted my cheek. "I don't think you are as unscathed by Mr. Hyde's actions as you think you are."

My throat tightened and I lowered my head so she couldn't see my tears. I wanted to hug her and be held by her, but we were in a public place and it wasn't the done thing.

"Oh, Emily."

"I don't love him," I said, dashing the tears away. "But I *had* decided to make a life with him. I suppose that's why I can't be angry at him for doing the same with that girl. He doesn't love her, but he will be good to her, I know it. Just as I would have been a good wife to him. I had settled it in my mind. Celia, I meant what I said yesterday. Theo was going to be my ticket out of my life as a medium. I don't want to perform anymore."

"I know." She rubbed my damp cheek with her thumb. "There will be other opportunities, Em, even if it means considering options we had previously discounted. We'll discuss it more at home. For now..." She nodded past my shoulder. "This room is no longer very private."

"Let's see if Adelaide is free." We wove through the crowds beginning to make their way into the refreshment room. The musicians were resting and the dancers thirsty. I spotted Adelaide across the room, talking to a footman. She saw us and waved us over.

"Emily, there's a woman here for you," she said. "A Mrs. Stanley. She said you'd know what it's about."

Mrs. Stanley! Finally. "Adelaide, I must apologize, but we have to leave."

"Does this have something to do with Lady Montgomery's governess?"

"Yes."

"And George's—I mean, Mr. Culvert's—absence?"

"Yes."

"Will you be all right? Will he?"

I laid a hand on her arm. She trembled. "Everyone will be fine. Don't worry. Go and enjoy your ball. Dance with all your admirers."

She wrinkled her nose. "I'm supposed to be dancing with Bertie, but I feigned a sore foot. I had better not dance with anyone or my falsehood will be undone." She kissed my cheek. "Goodnight, Emily. Goodnight, Miss Chambers. Good luck and be careful."

Celia and I collected our shawls from the ladies' dressing room and met Mrs. Stanley down in the servants' area out of the way of the busy maids and footmen.

"Bloody toffs," she muttered as she stormed past us.

Celia and I looked at each other.

"They think I am not good enough to be seen by them up there. I am no servant. I do not have to be shoved down here with the scrapers." This last she said loudly as we climbed the outside stairs to the street level.

The liveried footman standing at the bottom of the main steps glared at her then bowed at Celia and I.

"Mrs. Stanley," I said, drawing her away before she could rant at him, "how did you fare? You have the counter curse?"

She grunted. "I got it. Come. It is time to deliver it."

Celia instructed the footman to find George's carriage in the line of coaches waiting to take their masters and mistresses home. Drivers blew into their hands to warm them and huddled in groups chatting with other drivers or footmen. We waited until one of the carriages peeled off and circled Grosvenor Square to come and collect us.

A few moments later, we were rubbing our cold, gloved fingers together and traveling toward Mrs. Stanley's house.

Celia peppered her with questions all the way. Who would be there? What were Mrs. White's qualifications? Did the counter curse have to be delivered in such a diabolical method?

"Does *she* have to come?" Mrs. Stanley asked, having not answered a single question.

"Of course!" Celia snapped.

"I want her with me," I said. I wanted George and Louis too, but they hadn't returned. If they'd found the gypsies in time, they would have seen Mrs. Stanley fulfill her promise as we'd hoped and would be on their way back to London. I suddenly wished I'd told Adelaide where we were headed in case they showed up at the ball. Never mind. It would probably all be over before they arrived anyway.

We spent the entire journey going through the words to the counter curse. I spoke them aloud over and over, learning the subtle accents and nuances of the Romany language. It had to be just right, Mrs. Stanley said. By the time we reached Price's house, I had it committed to memory.

"Remember," she said as we alighted, "Mrs. Seymour—Mrs. White—thinks you are delivering the curse, although she thinks *you* are under the assumption that you will be speaking the words of the counter curse, which of course you will be doing." She wiped her brow with the back of her hand and lifted her gaze to a window on the first floor where light edged the drawn curtain. "It is best if you do not speak to her until after the entire procedure is accomplished. You do not want to accidentally mention that I am working against her. Not to her and not to Mr. Price. It is best if he knows as little as possible. It is safer for him that way.

Understand?"

"I won't say a thing," I said.

"Nor will I," Celia said. "But I don't like this."

"Then let's get it over with." I looped my arm through Celia's and followed Mrs. Stanley up the staircase to the small parlor. Leviticus Price sat in his usual seat by the window. His glacial blue eyes met mine and he nodded a greeting. "Nice to see you dressed for the occasion," he said. He did not get up, as a gentleman should, although that could have been because he was still too weak and not from poor manners. He did look exceedingly pale, his skin almost the same color as his drooping moustache and long beard. The only color in his face came from the dark shadows beneath his eyes, like semi-circular bruises. The two deaths he'd already suffered at the hands of Mrs. White had taken their toll. From the look of him, another would certainly kill him permanently.

Mrs. White entered from an adjoining room and stopped short when she saw us. "You're here," she said simply. "Good. We can start right away."

I had to bite my tongue to stop myself from telling her what I thought of her. This was the woman who'd killed Jacob, the woman who'd unleashed a demon and forced an evil spirit to possess my friends. She was an obsessed madwoman wrapped up in a homely package.

I hated her.

Celia's arm tightened around mine as if that would stop me from speaking my mind. But she needn't have worried. I would not jeopardize the task at hand. Not for all the anger burning within me, not for the revenge I longed to get on Mrs. White. Not for anything. Jacob's future came first. There would be time for all of that later.

"All will be well, Miss Chambers," Mrs. White said in the kind voice that I'd heard so many times. "Do not be afraid."

"There's been a change of plan," Celia said, letting go of me.

"What do you mean?" Mrs. White said.

"Celia?" I grabbed her by the arms and shook her when she didn't answer me. "I *must* go through with this."

"*You* don't have to do anything," she said. "I'll do it. I'll speak the words of the counter curse."

"No," I said. "This is my task."

"Your sister is right," Mrs. White said to Celia, but she looked at Mr. Price as she spoke. "Tell her, Leviticus."

"I've been up there," he said. His voice was scratchy, raw. "Miss Chambers, it's a confusing place, dazzling. The spirits speak to you, but you cannot yet understand them fully. She can. She will be less confused and will complete the task much faster than anyone else. I'm sure of it. The sooner she is done, the sooner she can be brought back."

"I *want* to do it," I said to her. "I need to see Jacob for myself. I need to...to say goodbye." That's if he was still there.

Celia pulled me out to the landing. Mrs. Stanley made to follow us but when she saw we weren't leaving, she remained in the doorway where she could see us but not hear our conversation.

"What if Mrs. White refuses to bring you back?" Celia whispered. "How can we make her if she won't do it?"

"She will. She wants to punish Jacob, remember? How best to do that than keep he and I apart forever? I in this realm and him...gone."

She shook her head. "I don't like it."

"Celia, I *want* to do it."

Her nostrils flared and her mouth turned down at the corners. She seemed to be battling to maintain composure. "I know. Just come back to me, Em."

"Oh, Celia." I hugged her fiercely and she held me for a long time. I felt her chest heaving as she fought to control her emotions. I wasn't sure who was comforting whom.

"We should hurry," Mrs. Stanley said, glancing back into the parlor. "She is growing restless. Do not worry, Miss Chambers. Together we three will make sure she brings your sister back."

I lay upon the sofa on Mrs. White's instruction. I felt strangely calm. My heart beat steadily, if a little fast, and my hands were clammy inside my long, white gloves, but otherwise I felt relaxed and ready. I was going to see Jacob and end his torment. That was the greatest incentive I knew to chase away fears.

Mrs. White opened a medical bag on the floor beside the sofa and removed a syringe. I closed my eyes. I didn't want to see her fill it, nor did I want to see Celia's reaction. She was terrified I wouldn't come back. I understood her terror, but there was nothing I could do about it. This had to be done. I didn't entirely trust a single person in that room except her, yet I had no choice but to go ahead.

Besides, I wasn't afraid of dying. If I never woke up after delivering the counter curse, I wouldn't regret going through with it. My only regret would be leaving Celia, Cara, and Louis behind because I knew they'd be sad.

Something cool touched my arm just below my shoulder. "Now, this will only sting for a moment," came Mrs. White's soothing voice. "Then you'll drift into sleep."

"No!" cried Celia. "I've changed my mind. Stop!"

My eyes flew open and I saw Mrs. Stanley holding my sister back. Tears streamed down Celia's face and dripped off her chin. "It's all right," I said as the needle bit into my skin. I gritted my teeth so as not to wince. If Celia thought me in pain, she would do anything to stop it.

"You have to let her go," Mrs. Stanley said to her. "This is so important to our future. You know it is."

"She'll be all right," Mrs. White said in her calm, even voice as she concentrated on injecting me with the lethal substance. "I will see to it she's brought back again."

"How can I believe you?" Celia said between her sobs. "Emily! *Emily!*"

I tried to smile, but I felt too tired to do even that. My limbs grew heavy and I couldn't keep my eyes open. I welcomed sleep as it folded me into its embrace.

"*Murderer!*" It was the last thing I heard Celia say. The last thing I heard anyone say.

I was drifting through a tunnel like a boat on a tide. It was dark, but a light shone up ahead. It grew brighter and brighter. I heard voices but couldn't make out any words. I think someone called my name but I might have been mistaken. The voices grew louder. They were shouting. My name rose above them all. I recognized the speaker.

"Jacob!"

"Emily, go back," he said. "Go back! You don't belong here. It's not your time. Go back!"

"I can't. Not yet." The counter curse. I began to chant the words I'd learned in the carriage. The light swirled above my head now, a huge whirlpool of brightness. A hand reached through and I knew it was Jacob's.

I faltered on one of the more difficult words and suddenly lost my place in the sequence. I had to start over. There was no time to berate myself. I began the chant again just as Jacob pulled me through the pool of light. His strong arms dragged me to my feet and held me against him.

"Hell, Emily! What are you doing here?"

I didn't answer him. I kept chanting.

He cupped my face and peered into my eyes. "Counter curse?"

I nodded.

He kissed the top of my forehead and shouted to one of the other spirits to get ready in case the lost ones returned. I glanced around, trying to take it all in yet not break the memorized sequence of strange words. We appeared to be in an enormous room. It had walls and rows upon rows of seats like a lecture hall. Well, what did I expect? It wasn't called the Waiting Area because it was a bath house.

But it was virtually empty. Aside from Jacob, there were only a handful of other spirits. Some were more transparent than Jacob, others mere outlines. They all looked terribly weak and weary.

Jacob held me as I spoke the final word. I'd done it! I'd said it perfectly, right down to the accent. I smiled up at him, relief flooding every part of me.

"It's over," I said. "We've caught Mrs. White and now you can cross. The Otherworld is safe."

Jacob pressed the heel of his hand to his forehead and stepped away. He doubled over as if in pain. One of the other spirits cried out and the faintest one disappeared altogether.

"Emily." Jacob shook his head but the action made him stumble. "Emily, you must go back."

"No. Not yet. I need to say goodbye to you properly."

"Emily...that wasn't the counter curse. They tricked you." He fell to his knees, clutching his head.

"Jacob!" I crouched beside him, my own head spinning, my stomach roiling. I wanted to be sick. "What have I done?"

He reached for me and held me close. "It's not your fault. Emily...go. How...?"

I shook my head, but that triggered a sharp pain slicing above my right eye. I buried my face in his shoulder and tried to regain a sense of myself, tried to think. It was so hard. Shards of ice ripped through my mind, tearing my thoughts out by their roots. All except one: Mrs. Stanley had double-crossed me. That meant she and Price were in on it too. There was no one except Celia to force Mrs. White to bring me back to life, and she could not to do it alone.

I was going to die.

A sudden blast of wind whipped around us, raking my hair loose from its elegant arrangement, whipping at my skirt with violent howls. It was so strong and I suddenly felt so weak. I would be blown away. More spirits disappeared, their cries lost in the tempest.

Jacob held my face in his hands and I knew how much effort that simple action took. I could hardly move. My head was a riot of pain and my body exhausted as I battled to stay.

"No, Emily, please not you." A single tear tracked down his cheek. "I don't want this for you."

"There's nothing we can do. I'm sorry. I'm so sorry."

"It's not...your fault." He kissed me. His lips were light as air but for the first time, I could actually taste him. I had never tasted anything so delicious, like honey and chocolate, but better. He broke the kiss and rested his forehead against mine. "You are my soul mate, Emily Chambers. I love you."

"I love you too." I had to shout it. The wind was so strong, trying to drag me in all directions, trying to break me apart and scatter my pieces. "Goodbye, Jacob."

We held each other as the gale screamed and roared, blowing the last of the remaining spirits into nothingness. There was just Jacob and I, and we could not hold on for much longer. I closed my eyes and buried my face in his chest. His arms held me against him, but soon even they loosened. I opened my eyes and was shocked by how transparent he looked. But it was me who drifted away from him, not the other way round.

"Emily!" His voice was no more than a whistle of wind.

"Jacob!" I tried to scramble back to him but the force pulling me away was too strong. I was sucked into the bright whirlpool of light again, then everything went still, quiet. The wind stopped. There were no voices, no sounds. I couldn't see anything except the light above but even that grew smaller until it was a mere speck.

Jacob. Where was Jacob? I tried to call his name but my voice didn't work.

Then suddenly even the light was gone. Snuffed out like a candle. I was surrounded by deep, blackest dark.

Nothingness.

CHAPTER 12

"Emily. Emily, wake up," Celia said. "Emily, can you hear me? Please, my precious girl, wake up."

"Here, let me try."

My body shook violently. It took me a moment to realize somebody else was doing the shaking. I opened my eyes, startling George who released me and stumbled backward.

"Emily!" Celia jerked me to a sitting position and threw her arms around me. "Be gentle," said Mrs. White. She stood behind me, but I recognized her voice. "She'll be weak for some time."

"Did you do it?" George asked, urgent. "Emily, did you speak the curse?"

I closed my eyes and held myself very still. I couldn't talk. If I did, I might break into pieces. I had delivered the curse that had destroyed the Otherworld. Destroyed Jacob. It was all so terribly, horribly *wrong*.

Someone in the corner of the room laughed. "You're too late." It was Price, but his laughter quickly ended. The sickening sound of bone smacking bone replaced it.

"Be quiet," growled Louis. "Do not give me a reason to shoot you."

Whimpering came from the same direction, out of my

sight. It was a woman, not Price. Mrs. Stanley?

"Emily, you must answer me," George said. His face and clothes were covered with mud, his hair a wild tangle. He'd been riding, I remembered. He'd gone to the gypsy camp with my father. "*Did you deliver the curse?*"

"I did." My whisper raked down my throat like sharp nails. God, it hurt. Everything hurt. "Jacob..." I tried hard not to cry. I wanted Celia to comfort me, but she was suddenly not there anymore.

"We have to hurry," said George. "Mrs. White, are you ready?" He removed his jacket, waistcoat, and shirt, throwing them on the floor in a heap. I expected Celia to protest that he should not appear in such a state in front of me, but she was actually helping him.

The world had gone mad in my absence.

"Sit," Celia said, shoving him into a large armchair.

George was barely settled when Mrs. White jabbed him with the syringe. I watched, appalled, as his eyes closed slowly. Is that how I'd looked moments before? Like I was merely going to sleep?

"W...what's going on?" I could hardly form the words. Hardly think. My mind was numb, my body aching. Every bone felt like it had been ground in a mill, every vein opened until I'd bled dry.

But worse than the aches was the memory of Jacob, fading to nothing. It would haunt me until the day I died. That day had almost been today, but I had enough presence of mind to realize Mrs. White had saved me and brought me back to life. My sister had succeeded after all, although she had not done it alone.

"Mrs. Stanley tricked you," Mrs. White said to me. "She and Leviticus."

"I know." My voice sounded thick, hoarse. "I'm sorry, I thought it was you. But...George...?"

"We bought the counter curse from the Romany," Louis said. "It didn't cost us as much as we had expected. It seems they didn't like the thought of the Otherworld not being there when they die either."

I remembered what Mrs. Stanley had said, about her people respecting death and the afterlife. It seemed she did not respect it as much as her tribe, or perhaps something else was stronger than her beliefs.

I turned a little to see Louis watching Price, the pistol pointed at his chest as he sat like a statue, his face stony. Mrs. Stanley stood at Price's side, her hand on her lover's shoulder. She did not look at me, but Price's cold gaze didn't waver from mine. Louis was as muddy as George and looked just as exhausted, but he glanced back at me and smiled reassuringly, although it wasn't reflected in his eyes. Worry had settled there. Worry and grim foreboding. I wished I could smile back to thank him for his efforts, but my heart was too sore. If George didn't succeed, if it was too late to deliver the counter curse, I would never smile again.

"That should be long enough," Louis said. "Bring him back."

Mrs. White had been busy filling another syringe. She injected the clear liquid into George's arm.

Nothing happened.

"He's not coming back," Mrs. White said, panic making her voice shrill. She tapped his cheeks but George's head lolled to the side, lifeless.

Price snickered. "He can't. The curse worked. It's too late for him now. You did it, Miss Chambers. You destroyed your lover and sent your friend here to his own destruction. Congratulations."

I turned my face into the sofa cushion. I was too exhausted and too heart-sore to cry. A great hole opened up in my chest and sucked all my energy into it. It felt like I was caving in on myself.

"He's coming back!" cried Mrs. White.

"Mr. Culvert," said Celia. "Mr. Culvert, can you hear me?"

He moaned. I turned to watch and held my breath. The air in the parlor grew dense as we waited for him to regain consciousness.

Then out of the corner of my eye, I saw something move so fast it was a mere blur. Louis shouted in alarm. Mrs. Stanley shouted too, but in a foreign tongue. She had the pistol, snatched from Louis' hand while he was distracted. She pointed it at each of us, yet none of us, her hands shaking. She uttered something in Romany over and over, interspersed with the very English and very angry, "Stay back or I will shoot."

My father didn't heed her. He lunged.

She screamed.

The gun went off.

I screamed.

"Louis!" Celia cried. "No! *No!*" My sister raced to him and grabbed him from behind, spinning him around. "Louis!"

He wrapped an arm around her and she burst into tears. His other hand held the gun. It was pointed at Price. A dark stain bloomed on Price's waistcoat.

"Leviticus!" Mrs. Stanley fell to her knees at his feet. "No!" She tried to cover his wound with her hands, tried to staunch the flow of blood. But it was no use. He was slipping away. "Save him! Do something. You!" she shouted at Mrs. White. "He is your husband, *do* something!"

Husband?

Price did not look at his lover as he died. He looked at me, an unreadable smile on his face. A moment later his spirit rose from the body and hovered near the ceiling.

"I wonder what awaits me," his ghost said, looking up. "Did your friend succeed, I wonder?" He did not sound afraid but curious and quite pleased with himself.

"If he didn't, you are going to become nothing," I said. "And if he did, then you will go to hell. Either way, I wouldn't want to be you right now."

He swooped down and stood in front of me, too close. I pressed myself back into the cushions, but he didn't try to hurt me. "It doesn't matter. I got revenge for my Fred.

Beaufort is dead. That's all that really counts. The rest would have given me satisfaction, but I'll settle for Beaufort watching you grow old from up there." He drifted off then disappeared entirely. For a brief moment I thought about summoning him back to ask him questions, but I didn't want to see him again. Good riddance.

Mrs. White touched Mrs. Stanley's shoulder as the landlady stared at her hands, smeared with Price's blood. "I'm so sorry," Mrs. White said. "I truly am."

I expected Mrs. Stanley to berate her, even curse her, but she did not. She surprised me by allowing herself to be comforted by the wife of her lover. I suddenly understood why she had set aside her gypsy beliefs to help him—love is powerful, and we are merely its mindless tools. She could no more stop loving Price than I could Jacob.

"Emily," Celia said, crouching beside me. "Emily, are you all right?"

"Of course." I sat up. "George?"

He waved weakly from his chair. "I did it, Em. I delivered the counter curse."

I couldn't breathe. My chest felt tight. He'd done it, but... "In time?"

"We'll have to wait and see."

We all looked to the ceiling, as if the Waiting Area was up above. Nothing happened. No spirits came.

Jacob...

"Tell me everything," I said. "Talk. I need to be distracted." At least until I knew for sure if Jacob was all right, or that he'd crossed over. I would not try to summon him. I dared not. Anyway, if the Waiting Area had survived, he may have crossed upon Price's death. "Price killed Jacob, didn't he?"

Mrs. Stanley emitted a single loud sob.

"He was my husband, Leviticus Seymour," Mrs. White said. I still couldn't think of her as Mrs. Seymour, married to that monster. It didn't seem right somehow. "I stopped loving him long ago, and he me." She watched Mrs. Stanley as she spoke, her arm still around the other woman's shoulders. "I had moved out of our family home but remained in contact, for Fred's sake. All contact ceased when Fred died. He killed himself." She shifted her weight but remained on the floor. She did not cry, not even a single tear, but the faraway look on her face told me she had not put aside her son or his death, and probably never would.

"Because Jacob wouldn't be his friend?" I asked. "I don't understand. Did Frederick not have other friends? And if he didn't and that is what pushed him over the edge, how is that Jacob's fault? He cannot be held accountable."

"I don't," she said. "At least, not anymore. At first I blamed him a little, but not now. Because, you see, it wasn't Jacob Beaufort's friendship he craved. It was his love."

I blinked at her. My sister gasped. Even Mrs. Stanley stopped crying and stared at Mrs. White.

"You mean...he was in love with Jacob?" I asked. "A forbidden love?"

"Good lord," George said quietly. "He loved men."

"Not *men*," Mrs. White said. "Man. One. Jacob Beaufort. He was obsessed, but neither Leviticus nor I knew it at the time. Not until after his death and we read his diary. It was all laid out in there. His private thoughts and desires, his attempts to get Mr. Beaufort to notice him, and his agony when he failed. Then his final desperate days when all he could think about was ending it all."

"How sad," Celia muttered. "How very, very sad."

"You say you were angry only at first," Louis said. "But your husband's anger lingered, didn't it?"

Her gaze slid to Price's body. She showed no emotion whatsoever. "Leviticus continued to blame Jacob Beaufort. He wanted him to suffer the way Frederick had suffered. He took his life, but it wasn't enough. He was still angry, so he decided to take his revenge out on those Mr. Beaufort loved. His family, then later, you, Miss Chambers."

"The amulet?" Celia asked. "Did you sell it to me?"

"Not me." Mrs. White nodded at Mrs. Stanley, who did

not look up.

"The disguise was excellent," Celia said. "Unfortunately." She picked up George's clothes and handed him his shirt.

"I didn't know anything about Leviticus's tactics until that night you came to the school and sent Mr. Blunt away. Indeed, I wasn't sure of his involvement until the next day when he came looking for Blunt and we spoke. I hadn't seen Leviticus for many months, since Fred's death. He'd gone mad in that time."

"He was not mad," Mrs. Stanley said, moving away from the comforting arm of Mrs. White. "He felt things deeply. The loss of his son hurt him. I understood that hurt. I lost a son too."

"I'm very sorry," Mrs. White said, but Mrs. Stanley turned her face away. I felt a rush of sympathy for her. She'd lost a son and now her lover too.

"If you weren't helping Price then, why help him now?" George asked. "Why do this to good, innocent people?"

"Innocents?" Mrs. White said. "You mean you and Miss Chambers."

"And the orphan who died after you injected him."

"That was a terrible tragedy." Mrs. White shook her head and tears welled in her eyes.

"What happened after that night Blunt left the school?" I asked. "You decided to leave too, but why not tell anyone where you were going?"

"I was afraid of Leviticus, of what he might do. My attempt to hide from him was for naught, however. He found me again last week and asked me to...kill him and bring him back to life." She screwed up her nose, as if the thought of what she'd done disgusted her. "He said he'd do it anyway and Mrs. Stanley here would bring him back. I couldn't let that happen. She has no medical training, but I at least have some. He already had the poisons and antidotes. He got the ingredients from the Society's storerooms but made the concoctions himself. He used to be a pharmacist. I believe he'd been experimenting for some time on rats."

"Hell," George said. "We do have medicines and poisons, for testing purposes. There are some members who believe they can cause hallucinations that bring one closer to experiencing supernatural phenomena, hysteria, that sort of thing. I had no idea they could be combined into such lethal substances, but I suspect others knew which is why these things are kept locked away. Price, as master, had a key. Damn."

"It's not your fault," Mrs. White said. "I didn't know what Leviticus was doing until after his first two deaths. When I pressed him, he told me about the curse. I refused to do it a third time. I told him it would kill him, which it would have done. So he found that poor child and..." She sniffed. "When that failed, he coerced Mr. Blunt into doing it. He held back the opium, which he'd been supplying for some time, and forced him to be my...victim. I didn't want to be party to it but Leviticus told me he'd kill Mr. Blunt if I did not help. When you interrupted us yesterday, Miss Chambers, I couldn't tell you what was really happening. I had to pretend we were giving Mr. Blunt a cure for his addiction. Leviticus warned me that if I told anyone the truth, he would kill Mr. Blunt then me. I believed him."

"Very wise," I said.

"After you left, Mrs. Stanley and Leviticus realized you may not have fallen for the ruse, so he sent her to your house to pretend to be a turncoat and point the finger of guilt at me."

"It worked," I said.

"Almost," George added, completely dressed once more although his tie was crooked. "Emily, I am so glad we didn't believe her entirely."

"A healthy dose of skepticism never hurt anyone," Louis said.

I attempted a smile. "You would get along well with Lord Preston."

"Leviticus was a good man," mumbled Mrs. Stanley into her hands. "He was...lost. Angry."

"It's all so sad," Celia said. "The loss of a child, or a loved one, can do terrible things to one's mind." She glanced at Louis. He rubbed a hand over his stubbly chin.

"There's something I don't understand," George said, frowning. "Frederick died months ago, and Beaufort soon afterward, correct?"

"Yes," said Mrs. White. Louis helped her to stand and guided her to sit on the sofa near my feet. He still held the pistol but kept it pointed away from everyone.

"Then why the long wait between then and now? The shape-shifting demon was summoned mere weeks ago. Why didn't he begin his revenge sooner?"

"Because of me," Mrs. Stanley said, lifting her tear-streaked face. "We met the day after his son died. I used to travel with a circus, telling fortunes. He came to me wanting answers and we became friends. I understood him, my situation being not too different from his. He was devastated, sick with unhappiness and disbelief and a burning rage. We just talked, and he was interested in my people and their beliefs concerning the dead. He came back the next day and said he'd read about gypsies and curses. He asked for a very specific curse, something that will destroy the spirit, not just the life. I knew he wanted to hurt the Beaufort boy, although I did not know his name then. It was clear on his face that he wanted revenge."

"So you gave him a curse!" I cried. "You just handed it over for a few coins!"

"I did not," she snapped. "Do not judge me, Miss Chambers. I was angry too. I wanted revenge for my own son's death, but I could not get it. I never learned who killed him. I wanted to help Leviticus, and I wanted to act on my own anger and sorrow through him."

"It is still a despicable thing to do to a stranger," Celia said.

"I did not kill him," she said. "Nor did I curse his spirit, not in the way Leviticus wanted. Something held me back. Fear, perhaps. I was brought up to leave the Otherworld alone, to respect it. But I knew the curses, just like all the custodians in my family do. So I gave him a more harmless one to use, one that would not destroy Beaufort's essence but send his spirit into a—what do you call it?—limbo, forever waiting."

"Is that not cruel enough?" White-hot rage burned inside me, bursting before my eyes, consuming me until it was impossible to think of anything else except my hatred toward Price and this woman.

Celia gripped my hand and Louis moved to my side. Two guardians, ready to protect me. Or stop me.

"You helped him summon the demon and then Mortlock much later," George said to Mrs. Stanley. He at least sounded calm, sensible. "You gave him the curses to destroy the Otherworld when it went against your beliefs. Why?"

"I did not see him again for months after I gave him that first curse. Then one day he showed up at my tent. We talked some more and I discovered that he needed a new home."

"So you offered Price these rooms?" I asked Mrs. Stanley.

"I left the circus and bought this house with money I'd saved and an inheritance. We moved in together and fell in love. I wanted to help him. I wanted to cure him. I thought if he had his revenge completely, he would get better. So I cursed the amulet and told him how it could be used to release the demon. He knew about possession himself, through his books, so Mortlock was all his doing, but I found that little girl."

"Cara," Celia whispered. She reached up and clutched Louis' hand.

"I'd seen her at the market in Leather Lane. One day she was talking to herself, and when I asked her who she spoke to, she told me there was a woman. There was no one there, but I did not doubt her. I knew she could see spirits."

"But neither the demon nor the possession assuaged Price's anger," George said. "You had to go one step further."

"He grew more angry every time you won." Mrs. Stanley looked at me but there was no malice in her eyes, just emptiness, as if all her anger and sadness were washed out by her tears. "He needed something more permanent, something to finish Beaufort forever."

"And you told him about the curse?" Louis asked. "Just like that? Did you not think through the consequences?"

"Of course I did. But he was so unhappy, and by then I would do anything for him. Anything. I was not afraid of becoming nothing myself. I welcomed it." She shrugged one shoulder. "I knew I was going to an awful place when my time came. Leviticus knew that too. Our crimes had already been committed, and there is no good place in the Otherworld for the likes of us. Why not destroy it altogether? What did it matter to us?" Her face crumpled, twisted, and a sob bubbled up from her chest. "Neither of us was going to be with our beautiful boys. I would rather be nothing than face never seeing my son again."

Her quiet sobs made the only sound in the otherwise silent room. She cut a lonely figure on the floor near the feet of Leviticus Price, her gray hair tumbling out of its pins and over her face. George rose but I did not get off the sofa. I felt stronger yet still so empty. Jacob had not come to me. He must have gone. I hoped he'd crossed over, that we'd not been too late.

At least I'd said goodbye.

"This must be reported to the police," Louis finally said. "We cannot hide the fact Leviticus Price was shot."

"We cannot tell them everything," Celia said. She seemed to suddenly realize she was holding Louis' hand and let go. She tucked it behind her. He stretched his fingers then balled them into a fist.

"We'll go to Lord Preston first and tell him what we've learned," I said. "If we can get him to believe us, he might be able help us to convince the police that Price was killed in self-defense." Getting him to change his mind was highly unlikely, but we had a duty to tell him who had killed Jacob.

If he did believe us, his influence would be extremely useful when it came time to inform the police.

I expected Mrs. Stanley to say something, but she did not. Mrs. White, however, nodded. "I will agree to say the same thing. There is no need for anyone here to suffer further."

"Thank you," my sister whispered, dabbing at her damp eyes with the edge of her sleeve.

"Emily, are you well enough to go home?" Louis asked. "Should I carry you?"

"I'm well," I said, getting up.

"Don't exert yourselves too soon," Mrs. White said to George and me. "You must rest."

"No problem there," George said, buttoning up his waistcoat. "I feel like I could sleep for a week. Come, Emily, we'll go to the Beauforts' together. Do you think the ball will have finished?"

I stood, but the room tilted and my legs gave way. I felt myself falling, but something caught me before I hit the ground.

Not something, someone. "Jacob!"

"Emily, you look terrible." His hands circled my waist as he gently lowered me to the sofa.

"He's here?" George asked. "Beaufort is back?"

"He is," I said. And he was holding me. It was exactly where I wanted to be, and where I wanted him to be. By my side.

"Em, are you all right?" He pushed the hair off my forehead and kissed me there. "Answer me."

"I'm all right," I said. "Oh, Jacob." I threw my arms around his neck and buried my face in his shoulder. I allowed myself one almighty sob then gathered my wits and drew back to look at him properly. He was almost back to the way he used to be. Although most of him was solid, like any living man, his edges were a little smudged, as if someone had run their thumb around him. I caressed his cheek, his jaw and neck, unable to get enough of him. It was so good to touch him again, and to know the danger to the

Waiting Area was over.

He closed his eyes and leaned into my hand. "Thank God, Emily. Thank God you're alive."

"The Waiting Area is back to normal?" George asked.

"It is," Jacob said, but there was a small hesitation in his voice.

I repeated his words for the others then said, "What's wrong?"

"I feel a little weaker than I used to."

"It may take time before you are fully restored to your usual spirit self." But there was more. He didn't quite meet my gaze and I knew he was keeping something from me. "Jacob? What is it?"

"As you can see, I haven't crossed," he said heavily. "I thought I would now that Price is gone. I saw his spirit briefly in the Waiting Area, but he didn't see me. It was him, wasn't it? He tried to destroy the Otherworld. He was the one who brought Mortlock back and the demon. He ended my life. So why am I still in the Waiting Area?"

"Oh, Jacob, I'm sorry. I wish I knew."

"I think it's something to do with what he said to me when I died. That I must give something up." He faded a little, not quite as much as when the Waiting Area was under the curse, but he certainly wasn't solid anymore. "Do you remember, Em?"

"I do. You still think that relevant now that he's gone?"

"Yes." He closed his eyes. "I feel so tired."

"You can rest soon." I cupped his face in my hands. "Think. What could you possibly have to give up?"

But it wasn't Jacob who answered me. It was Mrs. Stanley. "He must give up the one thing he truly cares for," she said. "But he cannot. Can you, Mr. Beaufort?"

"You know what it is?" I clutched at Jacob's arms. The muscles tensed beneath his shirt. "Tell me. I want you to crossover. I want you to be at peace. Tell me what you must give up and I'll help you."

His mouth twisted, his nostrils flared, and for a brief

moment he fainted away to almost nothing before flickering back into existence again. "It's impossible, Emily." His voice was thick with emotion and exhaustion. "She's right. I've tried. I tried to give you up. But I can't."

"Me?" I whispered.

"What is it?" Celia asked. "What did he say?"

"That he must give up me, yet..." I shook my head. We'd suspected that he had to stop loving me and let me go, but when he had tried, nothing happened. "It didn't work last time."

"That's because I couldn't do it. I couldn't give you up. Anything else, yes, but never you." The corner of his lips curved into a wry smile. "Not even for everlasting peace. I love you. Stopping is an impossibility."

I pressed my cheek to his heart but there was no beat. He felt so cold and he faded a little again.

"There is another way." I heard Mrs. Stanley's words, but they didn't sink in until Louis, George, and my sister prompted her for more. "Now that Leviticus is...gone," she added, "there is something else you can do. Is he weak, Miss Chambers?"

"Yes," I whispered. "Why? What is happening to him?"

"Please Mrs. Stanley," Celia urged, "make amends. Do the right thing, and tell us what to do."

She didn't answer for so long that I thought I'd scream with frustration. Louis adjusted his grip on the handle of the pistol, but he didn't use it to threaten her. I was afraid my sister would snatch it from him and do it herself if Mrs. Stanley didn't speak.

Thankfully the landlady did. "You must find Beaufort's body," she said. "And quickly. Now that the one who laid the curse on him is gone, Beaufort's body is dying."

"He's already dead," George said.

"No, he's not," she said. "He's still alive. But not for long."

CHAPTER 13

Alive? Jacob was alive?

Impossible. It had to be. Either I was dreaming or Mrs. Stanley was lying.

And yet...and yet...

"Why should we believe you?" George asked her. "You've lied so many times already. How do we know this is not one more?"

"It may be." Mrs. Stanley's accent seemed thicker and her manner was of someone who no longer cared what anyone thought. I felt a little sorry for her. I didn't understand why she could love someone like Price, but I understood deep, soul-wrenching love, and that was enough for me to forgive her role. "But you will not know for sure until you find his body."

"We have to trust her," Celia muttered. "We cannot risk doing nothing." She looked to me. Everyone did.

I clutched Jacob's shirt, even as he faded in and out. I didn't look up at his face. Could not. If I moved, if I spoke even in a whisper, I might shatter this dream and wake up into a nightmare instead.

It was Jacob who roused me. "Emily," he said urgently. "Emily, ask her where my body is. Ask her how she knows this. Ask her...bloody hell." He pressed his forehead to mine and breathed deeply, despite not needing air.

I pulled away and held his hand as if that could stop him disappearing. He shimmered but remained.

"You had better tell us what you know," I said, putting as much of a threatening tone into it as I could.

Mrs. Stanley sat heavily on the chair and smoothed her apron over her lap. She looked much older and somewhat weaker, as if all the life had gone out of her. "When Leviticus first came to me at the circus and asked for a curse to use on the Beaufort boy, I was hesitant. He paid me a large sum, but still, I did not like the idea. I was not in love with him then. I sympathized with his tale, but what he asked went against everything I was brought up to believe. I could not do it."

"But you took his money anyway," Louis said.

She nodded. "I gave him a curse that I told him would obliterate his victim completely. He would have no existence, not in this world or the Otherworld. All he had to do was make him lose consciousness, not kill him, then speak the curse."

Jacob let go of me and I thought he was going to fade away completely, so faint was he. But he sat on the floor, his back against the sofa. He clasped is drawn-up knees and stared straight ahead. I knelt beside him and touched his shoulder. He didn't move.

"The curse you gave Price...what did it really do?" I asked.

"It turned Beaufort into a spirit, separated him from his body. But he was more than a spirit, or perhaps less, depending on your point of view."

"He is more solid than other ghosts," I said, "and can go where others cannot."

"But he could not crossover, could never be truly dead unless he gave up what he loved most."

Me.

I tightened my grip on Jacob's shoulder. He did not acknowledge my presence. It was as if he wasn't even listening.

"Jacob said his killer told him that he must give something up," I said, "something he loved dearly."

"I did not want to dabble in the spirit world back then," she said. "So I gave the milder curse to Leviticus and told him to tell Beaufort that he had to give something up. It was my way of helping Beaufort end the curse himself and return to his body and his life, but I told Leviticus that it was merely a part of the curse and would not work if left out." She cast a longing gaze at Price's body. "I lied to him and I did not know how to end the lie."

"But Jacob couldn't do it," Celia muttered. "He couldn't give you up, Em." She stared at me, her eyes widened and filled with wonder.

"A man can never truly set aside the woman who occupies his heart," Louis said. "No matter how much distance or time separates them."

"Very true," George said.

Jacob took my hand and kneaded my fingers.

"So you never told Price the truth?" I asked Mrs. Stanley.

"He soon realized something was wrong when you poked your nose in. You claimed to be speaking to Beaufort's ghost and he knew you had no reason to lie. Leviticus blamed me for giving him the wrong curse. I told him it was innocently done, and he...he believed me." She wiped away the tears washing silently down her cheeks. "He decided to use Beaufort's spirit state to his advantage instead. He did not know that Beaufort was not really dead, see, and I never told him."

"So he thought he'd make Jacob's spirit suffer by watching his loved ones hurt," I said. "He set the demon onto Jacob's family and he summoned Mortlock into his sister's body."

"When that did not work, he wanted to end it once and for all by destroying everything, the entire Otherworld," Mrs. Stanley said. "He didn't care what would happen to himself anymore, and by then I loved him too much not to help."

"So you gave him the most dangerous curse there is," George said. "Mad. Utterly mad."

"Hush, George," I said. We needed Mrs. Stanley's help and blaming her was not going to win her over. "Mrs. Stanley, where is Jacob's body?"

"I do not know, do I? I was not there when Leviticus set upon him."

"You don't know!" I stormed over to her and grabbed her by the shoulders. "How can you not know? Why didn't you find out?" I was so angry I wanted to shake her until the answers fell out, but someone gently pulled me away. Two someones, I realized, Celia and Louis.

"We'll find him," George said. "Let's approach this scientifically."

"Emily," Jacob said. "Emily, it's no use. I can't do it. I can't give you up. And I'm so weak..."

I knelt in front of him. He closed his eyes and his face crumpled. "Be strong. You have to be. There must be a counter curse?" This I said to Mrs. Stanley.

She nodded. "There is. Find his body, speak the words, and his spirit will return as if nothing were amiss."

"You'll tell us what to say," said George. It was not a question but a demand.

"I will. If you do something for me."

"Name a sum."

"I do not want money," she said. "I want you to kill me."

Celia and Mrs. White gasped. George swore under his breath, but I simply sat back on my haunches and stared at her.

"I cannot do it myself," Mrs. Stanley said. "Taking my own life goes against my beliefs."

"As it is against ours for taking another's," Mrs. White said. "We cannot do it. I won't be a party to it."

"Then you can look the other way," George said bluntly. "We'll do anything required. Even that."

"Why?" Mrs. White asked her dead husband's lover. "You could have money, live comfortably."

"Because she wants to be with him," I said. "If you've never loved deeply, Mrs. White, you wouldn't understand."

She shook her head slowly. "You're right, Miss Chambers, I don't understand."

"You must hurry," Mrs. Stanley said. "Now that Leviticus is gone, the body will be dying. Beaufort's spirit will not last much longer."

"How much time have we got left?" I asked.

"Perhaps an hour, maybe two."

"An hour!" I felt like I'd been punched in the stomach. How could we find his body in an hour when no one knew its location?

To my surprise it was Celia who sprang into action first. "Jacob, do you know where you were killed, or cursed? Perhaps your body is nearby somewhere."

"It was in the country," I said, recalling an earlier conversation I'd had with him. "But his body could have been moved afterward for safe-keeping."

"Is there a basement to this house?" Celia asked Mrs. Stanley.

"Yes, but I can assure you there is no body in it."

"I'll look," Louis said and ran out the door.

Mrs. Stanley sighed. "You could try the Society."

"Of course!" George slapped his thigh. "I'll drive to the hall now."

"It would require utter seclusion," Mrs. Stanton said. George paused mid-stride. "Leviticus could not risk it being found."

"Hell. There's nowhere particularly secluded at the hall. We have other storage rooms, though. Small warehouses really. Beaufort could be in one of those, but—"

"Then let's go," I said, rising.

He shook his head sadly. My heart plunged at the pained look on his face. "Emily, there's so many, littered around the city. I don't know where they all are. Nor do I have keys."

"Price had keys. They must be here somewhere." I looked to his body, but Mrs. Stanley got there first.

"I'll search him," she said, lovingly unbuttoning his bloodied waistcoat.

"But even if we find them, how will we find the warehouses?" George asked. "How will we search them all?"

"Em, it's hopeless," Jacob said. He still sat on the floor, embracing his knees.

I knelt beside him again. "We have to try, Jacob. I will not give up without a fight. Not when there is a chance." I gritted my teeth and fought back the wave of hopelessness. "George, you must find out where the storage rooms are. Is there a member you can ask?"

He nodded. "Our second master. He lives not far from me."

"Drive us to Lord Preston's house on your way to the second master's home, then send word there once you have some locations. We'll split up and search them."

"If you can convince Lord Preston to help."

"We will." I was utterly determined to make Jacob's father believe us.

"But that will take so much time," Mrs. White said.

"Then we have to hurry. Mrs. Stanley?"

She had finished checking Price's pockets and was searching through the drawers of a desk. "Here!" she shouted, triumphant.

George took the keys off her. "Now, tell us the counter curse. Is it difficult?"

"Not very." She launched into the words one of us would need to speak if—no, *when*—we found Jacob's body. Unlike the counter curse that fixed the Waiting Area, this one was in English and was easy to remember.

"Let's go," George said when she'd finished.

I went to follow him, but Jacob caught my hand. "Wait." He picked up my shawl from where it hung over the back of the sofa and gently wrapped it around my shoulders. "Take care."

"You're not coming?" I asked.

His eyes turned wild and glassy, as if he wasn't quite

seeing things in our realm, but in the Waiting Area and beyond. "I have a better way. Faster," he said. Then he disappeared.

"Jacob!" I tipped my head back and searched the ceiling. George and Celia urged me to go with them, and so did Louis upon his return from the basement.

Precious seconds ticked by and Jacob didn't return. I followed the others out while Mrs. White and Mrs. Stanley remained behind. I wasn't sure it was a good idea leaving the two together but Mrs. White assured me she would be all right, and that she would notify the police about Price's death.

We ran down the stairs and George rattled off instructions to his driver. He certainly heeded the "post-haste" part because the horses flew through the streets back to Belgrave Square.

The ball had ended. There were no coaches outside Lord and Lady Preston's house, and no footmen either. Light shone from the upstairs windows. I ran to the front door, my sister and Louis behind me. George drove off to speak to the Society's second master. I banged on the door and it seemed to take a lifetime for the butler to open it. He loomed large and looked decidedly unhappy about the intrusion, but when he saw my sister and I in our ball gowns, he resumed his professional demeanor. He must have thought we'd left something behind earlier.

"We need to see Lady Preston," I said.

He bowed, but I didn't have time for such niceties. I pushed past him and ran up the stairs.

"Miss! Miss!" he yelled.

"Lady Preston!" I shouted. "Adelaide! We need you. Jacob needs you."

But it was Lord Preston who greeted me at the top of the grand staircase. With his thick, gray moustache and huge frame, he was as ferocious as an angry bear. But I would not back down. I couldn't afford to. He *had* to listen to me.

"Jacob needs your help, my lord," I said. "I know you

don't believe—"

"Enough!" he bellowed. "I have put up with this nonsense for too long."

"Actually, you haven't *put up* with anything. As I recall, you've been quite belligerent about it all."

"You are a disrespectful, malicious, and base-born girl. I should never have let you into my house tonight. It was a mistake. Now leave."

"Indeed it is enough," said Louis. His voice was a low growl, his jaw rigid as he stood beside me. "I don't care who you are, you will not speak to my daughter like that."

"Who are *you*?"

"I just made that clear. I'm her father. Emily has come here seeking help for *your* son. You owe her a great debt, sir."

"Owe? Her?" Lord Preston advanced down the steps, one at a time. "That is laughable. Get. Out. Now. All of you."

I held up my hands, but Lord Preston ignored the placating gesture. He continued to advance down the steps with menacing slowness, his strong brow deeply scored by his frown. "I know this is a lot for you to take in," I said, "but for just this once, set aside your beliefs. I know you're hurt, and I don't blame you for your anger toward me. But listen to me now, I beg you. If our plan doesn't work, you will never see me again."

"You're right, I will never see you again," he snarled. "Starting now. Polson! Remove them."

"Please, my lord." I glanced back at the butler. He looked uncertain as to the reaction he would receive from Louis. "If nothing happens after we find Jacob's body—"

"His what?" Lord Preston took a stumbling step back up the stairs. "You know where his body is? Tell me. *Tell me!* Where is it? How do you know?" He was advancing again, faster, coming at me with those big paws outstretched as if he would wrap them around my throat and squeeze the answer out.

"Reginald?" Lady Preston said from the landing above.

"Reginald, who—? Miss Chambers!"

"Lady Preston, there's so much to tell you. Please, you must listen to us. There's a chance we can save Jacob, but—"

"Where is his body?" Lord Preston shouted. He grasped my shoulders and shook me so hard my neck hurt.

Lady Preston gathered up the skirts of her ball gown and rushed down the stairs. "Reginald, let her go."

Lord Preston didn't heed his wife. Every shake grew more and more violent. Louis grabbed the lapels of the earl's exquisitely tailored coat and punched him in the jaw. Lord Preston tripped on the steps and landed on his rear near his wife's slippered feet. She gasped and knelt beside him.

Polson ran up the steps toward us, but Lady Preston ordered him to stop. "Fetch Adelaide. She's in her room. Everything is all right here." This last sentence was spoken to her husband who still sat on the step, his eyes unfocused, his shoulders stooped like an old man.

Polson glanced at Lord Preston then did his mistress's bidding.

"What were you saying about saving my son, Miss Chambers?" Lady Preston asked me. "Were you able to save the Otherworld?"

"Yes, but this is something else. Something more." I spoke quickly, the words spilling out like a waterfall. "Jacob is alive. We need to find his body to bring him back." At Lady Preston's stunned silence, I shook my head. "It's complicated. A curse was laid on him by the man who wanted to kill him, Frederick Seymour's father, but it was the wrong curse. It didn't kill him, just put him into a type of sleep where his spirit was separated from his body."

"So he's...alive?" She slipped to the side and I was afraid she might tumble down the staircase, but she simply sat heavily. Both she and her husband were as white as the marble steps.

"I'll explain more later, but for now, time is running out. Jacob's body is dying. We have to find it which means we'll need to separate. We'll also need your coaches, as many as

you have. George will be back soon to tell us where to go."
She sat there, staring at me, her eyes unblinking, her mouth
ajar.

Lord Preston looked equally perplexed. "My dear...could
it be true?"

"I believe her," Lady Preston said, sounding quite dazed.
"And if you have any hope left, then you must too."

"But how can I? It's too...ridiculous."

"Oh, Father," Adelaide said from the landing above us.
She too was still dressed in her ball gown, but her unbound
hair fell around her shoulders. "Put aside your stubbornness
for one moment and listen to your heart. I know you want to
believe, so just do it. Please. If not for Jacob, then for
Mother and me."

He turned to look at her. "You think I wouldn't do
anything for your brother? That I would throw away any
reasonable chance of finding him again out of
stubbornness?"

"I don't know what to think. Perhaps it's more pride than
stubbornness." Her lower lip wobbled and her eyes swam
with tears. "You and Jacob did not get along before his
death, and since then it only seems you want revenge
because you hate it that someone took something from you."

He craned his neck to look up at her as she stopped on
the step above him. "You think I care so little about him?
About you?"

"You certainly don't seem sad, only angry. The only other
time I've seen you this angry was when you were fleeced out
of a small fortune by that investor."

"Don't, Adelaide," Lady Preston warned.

"No," her husband said. "It's all right." He reached up a
hand to his daughter but she ignored it, and he let it fall
limply to his lap. "You're right, my dear. I haven't been the
best father, either before Jacob's death or after. I've been
blinded by the search for him. It occupies me constantly, to
the point where I don't know what time of day it is anymore.
I forget to eat, I can't sleep. It consumes me."

"And yet when the opportunity to communicate with him presents itself in the form of Miss Chambers, you refuse to believe her."

"Adelaide, what you're saying, what all of you are saying...it's beyond belief. How can it be real? Give me solid facts and I will listen to what she has to say."

She closed her eyes and shook her head. "I can't, Father. You're right. It defies logic. Yet Mother and I believe her nevertheless."

"I can explain it," Celia said. She gripped my arm and squeezed hard, a sign she wanted me to stay quiet. "There is a tribe of Africans where all the women can communicate with spirits." She proceeded to tell him about my origins and how the ability to see spirits had been passed down the family line to me. Lord Preston did not interrupt. He seemed riveted. I suspect the history was something he respected. It was an explanation of sorts, and all the more real for being written down. "Emily did not wish to be a medium," Celia said. "She doesn't want the gift. Indeed, we are closing our little business immediately so she can resume a normal life."

"Celia," I said. "We can't. We'll have nothing to live on."

She squeezed my arm harder. "We'll discuss it tomorrow. For now, there are more urgent matters. Mr. Culvert will be back soon with directions. Lord Preston, please issue orders to your drivers to have all the coaches at your disposal ready. It's likely we'll need to separate. Once you've done that, return to the hall and I'll tell you the counter curse."

But he did not get up. Instead, it was Lady Preston who rose. She called for a footman as she ran down the stairs, her skirts raised immodestly high to avoid tripping. Adelaide gave her father a sour glare then swiped away her tears. She followed her mother.

"As you can see, this search is going to happen with or without you, my lord," Celia said. "Having you join us will help, however it's not necessary."

He stared at the retreating back of his daughter. His drooping moustache twitched, but otherwise he didn't move.

He still looked bearish but not like a formidable one, but rather a poor, chained beast in a cage. Defeated. I felt sorry for him.

"Join us," Louis urged him. "If we find your son's body in time and the counter curse is issued, all will be well and you'll come to believe us. If we don't and nothing happens, then you've only wasted an hour of your evening and this will all be over. We'll never bother you again, or your family." He held out his hand.

Lord Preston bowed his head. I sighed. It was hopeless. The man could not set aside his stubbornness and pride, not even for an hour. Not even in the hope of seeing his son.

Louis lowered his arm. Lord Preston's hand shot out and grabbed it. Louis hauled him to his feet and clapped him on the shoulder as if they were old friends.

Celia and I followed behind them, but I stopped short as Jacob appeared. He was considerably weaker, almost entirely transparent. I bit my lip to stop myself crying out at the shocking sight of him.

Then he suddenly disappeared. I waited. Celia did too, aware that I'd seen him. Louis and Lord Preston continued down the stairs.

Jacob did not return.

I began to shake uncontrollably. What if we were too late? What if that was his last attempt to see me? The tears rolled down my cheeks, silent but unrelenting. We were so close...to lose him now would be unbearable. Celia wrapped her arm around me and held me.

Jacob flared into existence again and I whimpered with relief. "Em," he said in the whisper that must be all he could manage. "Em, sweet..."

I hugged him fiercely and kissed his lips, his throat, his cheek. He wasn't gone. Not yet. There was still time.

"George will be here soon," I assured him.

"Not..." He pressed the heel of his hand to his eye and faded in and out.

"Are you in pain?"

He shook his head but whether that was because he wasn't in pain or he didn't want to answer me, I couldn't be sure. At the bottom of the steps, Louis and Lord Preston had stopped to look back at me. I expected angry words from Jacob's father, but I received none. That was one powerful punch from Louis to finally knock some sense into his lordship.

"Got him," Jacob said.

"What do you mean? Got who?"

"Administrators...you a favor...help find my..."

"They're going to help us find your body? How?"

He shook his head again. "Not going to...have."

"They have *found* your body?"

"...asked Price."

"But he's crossed over."

"Administrators...access..." He shook his head and winced.

"Tell me later. Save your energy. So where is it? Where's your body?"

"...storage...Society...Paddington Station."

The front door burst open and crashed back on its hinges, quite a feat since it was solid wood. George waved a piece of paper in the air. "I have all the addresses of all the warehouses."

"Good," I said, charging down the steps. "Which one is near Paddington Station?"

George scanned the sheet. Adelaide hovered at his elbow, reading too. "Here it is," he said, pointing halfway down the page. "Why?"

"According to Price, that's where we'll find Jacob's body." I ran outside, not caring who followed. I gave George's driver directions and climbed into the carriage. George, Lady Preston, and Adelaide got in with me. As we drove off, another carriage pulled up and Celia, Louis, and Lord Preston set off in it.

Jacob had disappeared.

It seemed to take an age to get to Paddington, but it

probably only took ten minutes. Moonlight cast an ethereal glow over the empty streets but kept the lanes in shadow. I felt like I was in another world. This quiet, sleeping London was not the city I recognized.

We piled out of the carriage before it had completely rolled to a stop in a small street behind the station. A large warehouse rose before us, all grand arches and high windows. I held the coach lamp as George unlocked the door. Inside was a long central corridor with several doors running along both sides. George unlocked the fifth one on the left and it swung open on creaking hinges. The smell of dust mixed with something bitter and putrid wafted out. I covered my mouth and nose, but the scent had already lodged in my throat and nostrils.

"We'll split up," George said, removing another lamp from a hook near the door. Adelaide clung to him and either Lady Preston didn't notice or didn't care. She and I peeled off to the right as George lit the other lamp and moved to the left with Adelaide. Outside, the rumble of wheels on cobblestones announced the arrival of the second coach.

"Found anything?" Celia asked as she entered behind me.

Lord Preston held his lamp up high. I did too. The yellow light cast a circle around us and we assessed the area of our search. The storeroom was quite small with no other doors that I could see except for the one we'd used. Several tables took up most of the space and a cupboard occupied one corner. There was hardly a spare square of table surface anywhere. Jars, boxes, caskets, and odd paraphernalia were crammed together or piled on top of each other. There were microscopes and sharp implements, brass syringes and pipes, tubes with colored liquids in them, scales for weighing, coils of rope and chains hanging from the ceiling beams. And that smell—it burned my nostrils.

Somewhere to our left, Adelaide squealed.

"What is it?" Lord Preston forged his way toward her.

"It's all right," came George's voice. "She just saw something...unusual."

"She's not the only one," Louis muttered. He bent down to inspect the contents of a large jar. By the light of my lamp, I could just make out the head of some creature inside it, not human but not like anything else I'd seen either. My stomach rolled. Celia made a gagging sound. Beside the jar was another with what appeared to be a four-legged duck covered in fur, not feathers.

I turned away and tried not to look too closely at any more jars. "There doesn't appear to be many things large enough to store a body the size of Jacob's," I said. We quickly and methodically checked under the tables, in the bigger boxes and crates, but there was nothing even resembling a human body. There was only the cupboard left. It was larger than Lord Preston, rectangular and wooden with two doors side by side. Strange markings were carved into them, but I was too far away to make them out.

George fumbled with the keys, their jangle loud in the thick silence. We all watched. Waited. George struggled with the lock and passed the lamp to Adelaide so he could use two hands. The click of it unlocking was the signal for everyone to hold their breaths.

George opened the doors. Adelaide held the lamp up high and covered her mouth.

I rushed to them in disbelief. Perhaps if I got closer, it would all make sense. But it did not. My heart plunged to the floor, and I crumpled along with it.

"No!" I cried. "*No!*"

The cupboard was empty.

CHAPTER 14

"He must be here somewhere." Lady Preston stepped into the cupboard and knocked on the walls. Each knock grew louder until she was pounding so hard I thought the wood would crack. "Where is he?" She swung round and fixed me with a wild glare. "You said he'd be here! You told me my son was alive! *Where is he?*"

I looked around the storeroom, but we'd checked everywhere. There were no more rooms, no more boxes or cupboards, nothing. "I don't know." My legs were too weak to hold me, so I remained on the ground, dirtying my beautiful ball gown. I didn't care. Celia held me, but I hardly noticed her and I did not feel comforted in the least. "He told me it was here. Price lied."

"Come, my dear," said Lord Preston to his wife. "Let's go home."

I bent over and pressed my forehead to the cold wooden floor and cried until I ran out of tears. My body was wrung out, all the moisture squeezed from me. I had nothing left.

"Jacob," I whispered. "Jacob, come to me."

But he did not. Either he didn't have the strength, or he was already gone.

God, it hurt.

"Bloody 'ell, what a racket." The child's voice startled me into sitting up. A boy sat cross-legged on the floor beneath one of the tables opposite. He wore a cap over scraggly hair and a patched up coat with sleeves that didn't reach his wrists. His feet were bare and his face dirty. He was also dead. "You 'eard me?" he asked, surprised.

I nodded. "I can see spirits. Who're you?"

"Dan." He crawled out from under the table and stood. He was perhaps eight or nine, or even older. It was difficult to tell with children who lived on the street. So many were under-fed that they were smaller than others their age. And I was quite sure Dan was a street child. His clothes were rather a giveaway.

"Who are you talking to?" George asked.

"There's a child here," I said. "A little boy."

"Who you callin' little?" the boy demanded, arms crossed over his thin chest.

I apologized. "It's hard to see in this light. Did you die here?"

"Aye. Got killed, I did."

"Killed? You mean murdered?"

He shrugged. "It were an accident, really. They didn't mean to do it." Another shrug.

"They?" It all suddenly clicked into place. I knew who this boy was and who "they" were. My heart kicked inside my chest as if it had suddenly re-started. "A lady put you to sleep, didn't she? With a syringe? And there was a man with her?"

"The street urchin is here?" George came up beside me and lifted the lamp although he couldn't see Dan no matter how much light he cast.

"S'ringe? Like this it was." Dan indicated the size with his hands. "She poked it in me arm and I fell 'sleep. I were s'posed to say some words, but I couldn't r'member 'em. The lady said she'd bring me back alive, but nothin' 'appened. I been waitin' 'ere for 'em. Thought maybe she meant I had to wait awhile b'fore she'd do it. But they ain't come back."

"They're not going to, Dan," I said gently. "The man is dead, and so are you."

Behind me, Lord and Lady Preston's footsteps had halted. They'd stopped to listen. Celia, Adelaide, and Louis moved closer.

The boy stuck his bottom lip out. "So that's that then. S'pose I can go now." He looked to the ceiling. "What's it like up there?"

"Nice," I said. "They'll take care of you."

"Is there food?"

"There's everything you'll ever need. You'll never want for anything again." I took his hand and he jumped in surprise. Then his fingers closed over mine and he shuffled close. The poor boy trembled. For all his bravado, he was just a child about to go on a strange journey alone. "Dan, have you been here in spirit form when the man, Price, has returned?"

"He come once to check on that body."

"Body?" I whispered. "What body?"

"The one under there." He indicated the floor where he'd been sitting.

"Is it a man? A young man, tall?"

He nodded. "Dark hair, trousers, and a white shirt. When I first found it, I talked to 'im, but 'e didn't answer back. Must be dead too."

I put the lamp down and rushed to the table and pushed. George and Louis joined me then Adelaide and Celia. We all pushed and the table crashed into the one next to it, knocking over jars and implements. I got down on my knees and scrabbled at the edges of the boards, but they didn't budge.

"Here." Lord Preston loomed over me, a chisel in his hand. He wedged it under one of the boards and cranked it. The board lifted and I ripped it all the way up as he moved on to the next one.

We all crowded around, lifting boards, tossing them aside. Slowly, slowly, inch by inch, Jacob's body was revealed.

"It's him!" I cried when I saw his face.

"My boy." Lord Preston dropped the chisel. His wife was on her knees, stroking Jacob's cheeks, her tears falling into his dirty hair.

I shut out the sounds of tears and gasps of wonder, and concentrated on the words Mrs. Stanley had made us all recite. There wasn't even time to pray that we weren't too late. "*Come back to us,*" I chanted and touched Jacob's hand as she'd instructed me to do. "*Return to this your body.*" The body twitched as if he were waking from sleep. My heart raced, but I did not allow myself to hope. Not yet. "*Draw breath.*" Jacob's chest rose and fell as he took a deep breath. "*Heart, beat.*"

Adelaide put her ear to his chest. "It beats!"

"My God," Lord Preston muttered, taking hold of Jacob's other hand. "My boy."

"*Wake up,*" I finished, "*and live.*"

Jacob's eyes opened. He blinked. The fingers on the hand I was holding clasped mine. Then he smiled. "Hello, everyone. Nice to see you again."

His mother sobbed into his shoulder and had to be gently removed by Adelaide so that Jacob could sit up. He hugged his mother and sister then finally his father. Lord Preston's shoulders shook and he held his son for a very long time. I wanted to let the four of them enjoy their reunion and tried to step back, but Jacob would not release my hand. His grip tightened.

I looked around at my sister and father, at George. There wasn't a dry eye in the room. Even the boy spirit looked emotional, although he could not cry with either sadness or happiness anymore. I beckoned him over and he knelt beside me.

"Thank you." I kissed the top of his head.

He smiled. "I was waitin' for 'im to come back, that man what killed me." He shrugged. "He's gone, you say?"

"He is."

He sighed. "No point me stayin' then."

"Is there anything I can do for you here?" I asked. "Anyone I can talk to who may want to know what happened to you?"

His mouth twisted in thought. "Tell my brothers and sisters what 'appened. They might be wonderin'."

"You have brothers and sisters?"

"Not real ones. They're orphans, like me. We stick togever, we do. Did. They live in Cuttler Lane in the basement of a burnt out buildin'. Whistle short three times and they'll come to you." He smiled and doffed his cap. "Thanks, miss."

"Thank *you* for your help."

I watched him fade away until he was gone.

"Let's get you home," Lady Preston said to Jacob.

They helped him to stand and his father caught him when he faltered. His legs were weak and no doubt stiff after months of not being used.

"We'll send for Dr. Trentham as soon as we get home," Lady Preston said, holding Jacob. His father held him from the other side and between them they walked slowly away. My hand slipped from his and I folded my arms over my aching chest. I watched him go, wanting desperately to be with him, speak to him, hold him.

But I did not. He needed to be with his family. There would be time for us later.

"Lord Preston," Celia called. "The police must be notified. Mr. Price is dead, shot. It's unclear who did it," she said vaguely, "but I think it may have been by his own hand."

"I'll speak to the police in the morning," Lord Preston said.

"After we get our stories straight. I'll not have my family interrogated."

"I think we'll be able to leave them out entirely."

She thanked him and we watched them go. Only Adelaide hung back. She suddenly grabbed George and kissed him fiercely on the lips. He dropped the lamp and it went out. Thank goodness her parents were preoccupied and not looking.

Adelaide tore herself away then ran after them. George watched her go, a silly smile on his face. Louis picked up the broken lamp and chuckled.

"Young love," he said. "I remember that."

"So do I," Celia said, watching him from beneath her lashes. "It was so long ago."

"Not to me. It feels like yesterday." Louis swung the lamp and followed Jacob and his family out. We all did.

George locked the store room door then the larger warehouse door behind us. I watched as the drivers and footmen stared open-mouthed at Jacob. His father opened the coach door for him, but Jacob didn't climb the steps.

"Em. Emily!" He turned around. "Where is she?"

"Here." I hung back, but he beckoned me, so I stepped forward. "How do you feel?"

"Tired. Sore." He grinned. "I've never been grateful to feel so exhausted before. Feeling it means I'm alive."

I laughed and began to cry at the same time.

"Ah, Em. Come here." He leaned a shoulder against the coach for support and folded me into his arms. His heart beat strong and a little fast. His breath warmed the top of my head. He was alive. "Don't cry, sweetheart. My Emily. My savior." He buried his face in my neck and heaved a shuddering sigh. His body trembled and I tightened my hold around his waist, letting my tears soak into his shirt.

"Jacob," his mother whispered. "You're not a spirit anymore. People can see you. The servants..."

"Come, son," Lord Preston said. "You need to go home and rest."

"It doesn't matter who sees," Jacob mumbled. But he allowed his parents to draw him away. Lord Preston threw a coat around his son's shoulders and helped him into the carriage.

I was led to the Culvert coach by Celia, George, and Louis. Numbly, I watched the buildings fly past and waved farewell to George from my front door when we reached our house. Inside, it was quiet; Cara and Lucy slept. Celia took me up to my room and helped me undress.

"I'll fetch you a warm cup of milk," she said, tucking the bedcovers around me.

***

I didn't see the cup of milk until the next day when I woke up. It had gone cold on my dressing table. I put a shawl on over my nightgown and went downstairs. Cara was the first to greet me. She threw herself into my arms, laughing with abandon the way a child of her age should. I had never seen her so happy.

"Celia told me what happened," she said. "So he's alive? Mr. Beaufort is really alive?"

"He is." I could hardly believe it myself. It seemed too amazing. For the first time, I realized how Lord Preston must have felt listening to me spouting about spirits and the Otherworld. Believing the unbelievable feels a little like exploring a foreign country without either map or guide.

"Can we visit him now?" Cara asked. "Please, Emily. I want to meet him properly."

"Of course. Let me get dressed and eat my breakfast."

"Breakfast is finished. It's past luncheon."

I'd slept that late? "I'll see what Lucy has in the kitchen."

I found Celia in the kitchen too. Lucy hugged me and passed me a bowl of soup. "I'm glad you're awake," my sister said. "You'll be having a visitor soon."

"Who?"

"Mr. Moreau. Louis."

"I suppose he'll be leaving for the colonies now."

"Yes. Finish your soup then I'll help you dress."

Celia hummed as she tightened my corset, which I thought was rather sadistic. Indeed, I had to order her to loosen it so I could breathe. She arranged my hair and helped me into my best green day dress, the one that hugged my hips and sported a neat bustle at the back.

"Only you could get away with that color," she said,

admiring her handiwork. "First, let's go downstairs to see Louis. Then it's off to see Mr. Beaufort for you." She kissed my cheek and smiled.

For once I didn't mind that she was playing matchmaker.

Louis waited for us in the drawing room. He took my hands and made me sit on the sofa. Celia sat on my other side. I felt like a book squeezed between two bookends.

"Emily, there's something we need to tell you," he said. "Actually, it's something Celia needs to tell you. I'm just here for support."

"Oh?" I looked from one to the other. My sister didn't meet my gaze.

"Celia," Louis prompted, his voice stern.

"I'm not sure how to begin," she mumbled into her chest.

"Start at the beginning," I said.

"Very well." She blew out a breath and met my gaze. "I am your mother."

"What!" I spluttered.

"That was not the beginning," Louis scolded.

I stared at her. Then at him. Then back at her. "I...I don't...oh. Yes. I do." My chest constricted. My vision blurred. I couldn't breathe. "You tied my corset too tight." *And you're my mother!*

She placed her hand to the back of my neck. "Calm down, Emily, this is no time for hysterics."

"I am not being hysterical. I have just discovered that my sister is my mother and my mother is my grandmother. I'm so confused. Are you still my father, Louis?"

He kissed the top of my head. "I am. Your mother...Celia and I fell in love when she was only sixteen."

"So it *was* love?" I asked. "Between the two of you?"

"Of course." He looked at her. I switched my gaze to Celia too and watched her struggle to contain a blush and fail.

"Yes," she said quietly. "It was. I never loved another like I loved Louis. He changed my entire world, made me see things differently, made me feel special. And then he went away, just as I discovered I was with child."

"Bad timing," Louis said, heavily. "The worst."

"Mama decided she would bring you up as her daughter. She didn't want my prospects ruined, or have me suffer the scandal. Unfortunately she suffered through the whispers and stares that were meant for me, but she was strong. So much stronger than me."

"You were only sixteen," Louis said gently.

"Emily is only seventeen and look what she's had to contend with." She sighed. "Mama bore all the scandal with a smile on her face, and loved you like her own. She was a better mother than I could have been. I wasn't ready, certainly not in those early years."

"I never felt unloved," I said. After meeting that boy Dan, and Cara of course, I knew how lucky I was to have people who loved me. My family might be unconventional, but I never lacked anything. In a way I had two mothers, and now I had a father too.

"No wonder you were upset with Louis for not writing," I said.

"As she ought to be," he said. "If I'd known..."

"It must have been a shock when he returned suddenly." I was just beginning to realize how much of a shock. She'd thought he'd died or given up and found another woman in the colonies, but to find out he was alive and still in love with her must have been quite a tumultuous experience.

"I told you I loved your mother," Louis said. "That wasn't a lie. I loved her—Celia—but I became ashamed of my circumstances. I wanted to do better for her. I wanted to *be* better. A prisoner with no money to his name in a far off land is not a good prospect. I couldn't ask her to wait for me."

"I wouldn't have cared," she said.

"Perhaps. Either way, your mother wouldn't have let you come to me if she'd known how far I'd fallen. And I have my pride too. It's not just men like Lord Preston who want the best for their loved ones, it's us ordinary folk too."

"What you or Lord Preston thinks is best, is not always what *is* best," Celia said, huffily.

"So what now?" I asked. "Are you going back to Melbourne?"

"Soon," he said. "I can't stay here, Emily. I'm sorry. I know you won't come with me. Your life is here with Jacob. I wouldn't take you away now. But your mother...I hope she will return with me. And Cara too."

My mother. It sounded so strange. To think, yesterday I had a sister and no mother, and today I had no sister but a mother. Whatever would I discover next? "Do I have to call you Mama?" I asked her.

"Only when you're ready." She nudged me, an impish smile on her face. It wasn't at all like a mother should behave, but very much as an older sister would. I wondered if I could ever think of Celia as a daughter ought.

"So you're going to leave?" I asked her.

"I don't know." Her smile faded. Her fingers twisted in her lap. "We've talked it through, Louis and I, but I need time to think about it."

"So you care for him still?"

"I never stopped."

Well, she'd hidden her feelings well. I thought she hated him.

"I need to see you settled first," she said.

Settled with Jacob. "It's late," I said. "I want to see Jacob." I began to rise but Celia's firm hand on my arm stopped me. "Emily." She glanced past me to Louis.

I swiveled to face him. "What is it?"

Louis patted my hand but I could see something troubled him too. "Now that it's all over, and their lives are returning to normal, there's a chance you may not be welcome at the Beaufort household."

"But...why?"

"Jacob is nobility," Celia said. "Goodness, they don't even want their daughter to wed your friend Culvert and he's rich and comes from good stock. They'll want a grand match for

Jacob, not..."

"Not a girl like me," I finished for her. Melancholy swept over me, and fierce longing too. Everything inside me ached. I had to see Jacob and hear from his own lips what he wanted. If I had to fight for him, I would.

***

I did not see Jacob upon arriving at his Belgrave Square house. We were shown into the drawing room by Polson and greeted by Mrs. Stanley and George.

"Emily!" George went to hug me but recalled his manners at the last moment and kissed the back of my hand instead. "I've just got here myself. Mrs. Stanley too."

She sat very still on a chair, her reticule in her lap, her dark gaze returning mine with defiance. "I have come for my payment," she said with a thrust of her long chin.

"Payment?"

"Yes," George whispered. "You recall what it was."

I went cold. I remembered. She wanted one of us to kill her. "I...I don't think...Mrs. Stanley, it's all over now. Please, do not ask us to follow through on the promise we made under such desperate circumstances."

"None of us wishes you the fate you wish upon yourself," Celia added.

"You promised!" She growled and bared her teeth, and all of a sudden she went from mild, middle-aged woman to a snapping, wild beast. "You said you understood." This she said to me. "You, of all people, *should* understand. I don't want to be here. Not without him."

"What does she mean, *you* should understand?" Celia asked me.

"Nothing," I mumbled.

"Tell them how it felt up there when you delivered the curse," Mrs. Stanley sneered. "Tell them how you wanted to stay with him, dead, and not come back here."

"But..." Celia dragged on my shoulder, spinning me round to face her. But I could not look her in the eyes. "You came back. She came back," she said to Mrs. Stanley.

195

"I said she *wanted* to stay there, not that she did or could."

"Emily..."

"Don't, Celia. It's over. What's important is the next chapter of our lives." I didn't want to tell her I'd wanted to die. She wouldn't understand.

"You are with your loved one, Miss Chambers." Mrs. Stanley said, approaching me. "Now it's my turn to be with mine." She opened her reticule and pulled out a small pistol. "Take it. Aim true." She thrust it into my hand. When I hesitated, she added, "If you don't, I will put another curse on you."

Celia pulled me closer, half shielding me. "That's enough," Louis said. "Leave my daughter alone."

Mrs. Stanley's lip curled into a snarl. "*Go from this world.*" She pointed a bony finger at me. "*Go free, spirit, and leave this earthly body.*"

My skin tingled. My insides felt as if they were unraveling. "Something's happening! She's cursing me."

"Stop!" Jacob shouted from the doorway.

"*I set you free, oh spirit, never to return.*"

My head throbbed. The room spun out of control. My legs gave way and I crumpled like a ragdoll.

Someone caught me before I hit the floor. The pistol was removed from my hand.

The noise level suddenly rose, piercing me behind the eyes. Everyone was shouting at once, making it impossible to distinguish words. All except Mrs. Stanley's high-pitched, crazed, "*Be gone—*"

The gunshot punched a hole through the wall of noise. The following silence was almost as deafening.

Mrs. Stanley lay on the floor, blood seeping out of a bullet wound in her chest. It was the same manner in which Price had died.

"Is she all right?" That was Celia and I suspected she was asking after my health, not Mrs. Stanley's who was clearly dead.

Mrs. Stanley's spirit rose out of her body and hovered

nearby. "Thank you." She said it to Jacob, not me, and I realized he was holding the pistol. He'd shot her. Mrs. Stanley nodded once then vanished.

Celia knelt in front of me, flapping her hand at my face. "Emily, can you hear me?"

"Y, yes." I sat up. Jacob pushed the hair from my face and kissed each of my eyelids tenderly.

"What in blazes was that?" Lord Preston bellowed from the doorway.

"I shot her," said Jacob. "She was going to kill Emily."

I opened my mouth to protest, but at Celia's whispered "Hush" I shut it again.

"Bloody hell," Lord Preston muttered.

Through the thick fog clouding my head, I heard George and Adelaide, Lady Preston too. Everyone was there. Jacob was there. Holding me, rocking me. He didn't speak.

After several minutes, his mother's gentle voice sounded close to my ear. "Let her go, Jacob."

He shook his head. I breathed in a deep, shuddering breath. "Never."

I pulled away and extricated my arms from his embrace. "I'm all right, Jacob. I'm here." I wiped his tears away with my thumbs, but I did not try to stand. I liked being there with him, so close together. Liked it very much.

"I don't care what people say," he whispered. "I don't care what you do." This he said to his father. "I will not give her up. Cut me off, disinherit me, it doesn't matter. I've been given another chance and I will not waste my life with someone I don't love. I love Emily, and I'm going to be with her."

Lord Preston cleared his throat and stretched his neck. His impressive whiskers twitched. "Well," was all he said.

"We can't," his wife said. She was still on her knees near us, her pretty face etched with concern. She looked much older. "We can't do this to him. Not now."

Lord Preston nodded slowly, thoughtfully. "But she will have to give up her séances."

"That certainly won't be a problem," I said.

"And we'll have to gloss over your family origins when our friends ask," Lady Preston said with a somewhat apologetic wince in Celia's direction.

"I won't deny who my parents are," I said.

"Stop putting conditions on it, Mother." Jacob rose and helped me to stand. My legs still felt weak but he tucked me into his side and I felt safe. "She will marry me, and that's final."

"You could tell everyone her parents are from the colonies," Celia said. "Louis and I are leaving for Melbourne soon anyway, so it wouldn't be a lie. Tell them her father went there to make his fortune many years ago and now he has." She smiled at Louis and he smiled back. "Tell them whatever to want."

"We could say he holds an important position," Lady Preston said, thoughtful. "Communication between the colonies and England is scarce at best. A good plan, Miss Chambers."

"Mother," Jacob chided.

"It's not for our sakes, dear, but for Emily's. The less speculation there is about her family, the easier it will be for her to fit into your life."

"What are the prospects like in the colonies?" Lord Preston asked Louis. "Any projects a man can sink capital into?"

"A man of capital could do very well there," Louis said. His eyes twinkled with new vigor. "Melbourne is a thriving settlement and more permanent buildings are going up all the time."

"Come into my study and we can discuss it further. Perhaps we can strike more than one arrangement between families today."

"Wait a moment, Father," Adelaide said. She took George's hand and he trailed behind her as she raced after her father. He stumbled then recovered and pushed his glasses up his nose. "If Jacob marries whomever he chooses, then so do I. And I choose George."

"We'll discuss it later," Lord Preston said.

"We will discuss it now."

"Father," Jacob said on a sigh. "At least listen to her. Culvert is a good man. You won't find better, and we owe him a great deal."

"You don't owe me anything, Beaufort," George said. "I certainly wouldn't accept Adelaide as payment."

"Hush," Adelaide said. "Marriage is as much a financial arrangement as anything else. If Father wants to give me to you as thanks, then we'll accept it."

"If you say so."

I looked to Jacob and he winked at me as he tried not to smirk.

Adelaide kissed her brother's cheek. "Thank you."

Lord Preston surprised us all by folding Adelaide into an embrace. "It seems my study is about to become very crowded. Come with me. Jacob, take Emily into the breakfast parlor where you can be alone. I'll send the servants in to clean up this mess."

I watched them leave, tears clogging my throat. I felt utterly undeserving of such love, but grateful for it anyway.

Jacob took me into the adjoining smaller parlor and closed the door. His breathing made the only sound in the room. I'd never heard anything sweeter.

He touched my chin and I looked up at him. He was smiling openly, such a rare and precious sight. "I shouldn't be allowed to be this happy," he said, the smile slipping a little.

"Don't say that. What happened to Frederick isn't your fault."

"It was in a way, but I won't jeopardize my future happiness because of a past mistake." His nod was emphatic and final. "If I learned anything from this whole experience it's that life is worth living. Even the bad parts. Indeed, the bad only makes the good seem so much better." He hooked me round the waist and reeled me in. "And you are so very,

very good."

He kissed me, hard and hungry at first, like he couldn't get enough. Then it softened and I wallowed in the warmth of his lips, the taste of his tongue, his smell, all the things I'd wanted to experience but couldn't when he was in spirit form.

He broke the kiss and kneeled down on the floor.

"Jacob, are you all right? Do you still feel weak?"

He grinned. "I am better than I've ever felt." He sobered and the blue of his eyes intensified as his gaze locked onto mine. "Emily." He took my hands in both of his. My heart skipped madly in my chest. "Before you, I was lost," he said. "Whether in this realm when I was alive, or in the Waiting Area, my life was only half-lived until you came along and filled it. You were the only light in my dark world, a calm island in a raging sea. You changed everything. You changed me. And now I want you to complete me by being my wife."

I got down on my knees too so that we could be level with each other, and because I couldn't stand on my wobbly legs any longer. I kissed his hands then let go to touch his chest where his heart beat a rhythm as fierce as my own.

"Please say something," he whispered. "Say yes."

I lifted my gaze. Smiled. "Yes."

He circled my waist and gently lowered me onto the thick carpet then kissed me so thoroughly, my body went limp. When we separated for air, I pressed my palm against his heart again. Still beating. I think I would be checking it for the rest of our lives.

He made to kiss me but I held him off. "We should stop," I said, breathless. "Someone might come in."

"Let them. I don't care. I want everyone, including the servants, to see how passionately in love I am with my fiancée."

I stretched my arms around his neck. "Indeed? Well then, you'd better kiss me again. We wouldn't want anyone to be in any doubt."

He did.

EPILOGUE

The ball held in honor of Jacob was a hastily thrown together affair, coming only seven days after his return to life. Not that I, or any of the other hundred people in attendance, could tell. It seemed to run as smoothly as an event planned months in advance. Indeed, the only great difference to Adelaide's coming out ball was that everyone swamped Jacob upon first sight.

I couldn't blame them. They had a great many questions for him, and he answered most as best he could without touching on the supernatural circumstances. This meant that many of his answers consisted of "I can't recall." Everyone knew, however, that his killer had taken his own life, something Lord Preston made very clear. His booming voice could be heard over the throng of conversation and music, the note of pride and affection for his son evident to all.

I watched Jacob and his family from the center of the ballroom where I danced with George twice and Wallace Arbuthnot once, although my toes regretted the decision to encourage the latter onto the dance floor.

"He cuts rather a splendid figure," Theo said, as we stood at the edge of the ballroom after dancing a polka together.

His eyes twinkled merrily but a hint of regret threaded his tone. "It's no wonder you fell in love with him."

"Everyone seems to adore him," I said as Jacob tipped his head back and laughed. He'd been laughing most of the evening and I was utterly mesmerized by the rich sound of it. He'd hardly laughed at all when he was a ghost, and certainly not with such abandon. What made it even more special was that he was laughing along with George and a thin fellow with floppy hair and a pronounced limp. I'd met him earlier and the youth had been so awkward around everybody that he'd blushed whenever he spoke. Now, with Jacob, there wasn't a blush in sight and they were like two old friends. Jacob was certainly making good on his promise to take notice of everyone.

"Emily." Theo's voice was a low murmur intended to be heard only by me. He bent his head down to be closer to mine and his fingers brushed my hand. "Beaufort is so popular, so...*available* to everybody, and I know you prefer not to be noticed. Being with him, you will be stared at more than I think you'll like."

I clasped his hand, because he seemed to be in need of reassurance, and gave him a smile. It was easy to do. Like Jacob, smiling and laughing was something I did a lot of lately. "You're mistaken. I don't mind being looked at *if* there is no offence meant. Curious stares I can cope with, distrustful and mean-spirited ones I cannot."

Those sort still existed of course. A week in Jacob's company wasn't enough to wipe them out entirely. Even at the ball there was the odd hurtful whisper about my exotic looks and I heard more than one matron ask her friends if I'd been a true medium or a fraud.

"Will you be happy with him?" Theo asked, rubbing my knuckles with his thumb.

It was much too intimate a gesture. I pulled away and glanced in Jacob's direction. He was watching me, his jaw rigid, an unmistakably possessive gleam in his eye. He bowed to his companions and strode through the ballroom toward us. The crowd parted for him and didn't hide their curiosity about his destination. We had not announced our engagement yet—a speech was scheduled for later—and we'd spent much of the evening apart since he was far too popular for me to get within three feet of him.

"Theo, I am the happiest girl in this room. Perhaps in the country. And you?"

He scanned the faces of the dancers and his gaze settled on one in particular. Suzette. "I will be," he said with more determination than one should need when looking upon one's fiancée.

"Excuse me, Hyde," said Jacob, squaring up to him. He bowed. "I need to dance with Miss Chambers."

A strange hush snuffed out the surrounding conversations. All heads swiveled like sunflowers turning toward the sun. Those close enough to hear him speak had already repeated his words to those behind them, making special note of his "need" to dance with me. Within seconds the whole ballroom must have known about it, if the ripple of conversation was any indication.

I felt like I was on display as I put my hand in Jacob's big one and let him lead me onto the dance floor for a waltz. I wasn't yet used to the attention, and contrary to what I'd said to Theo earlier, I was unnerved by it.

As if sensing my apprehension, Jacob held me tighter and we whirled around the other dancers. The wide skirt of my borrowed gown floated around my ankles like a cloud. There had been no time to have a new outfit made and Celia refused to let me attend in the same one I'd worn to Adelaide's ball, so Jacob's sister had graciously loaned me one of hers. The hem required adjusting but it was otherwise an exquisite dress of white satin with silvery lace and little lavender bows sewn into the fabric.

"Jacob, are you all right?" I asked. "You feel a little tense." Indeed, his shoulders were like bricks and his back was ramrod straight. He stared over the top of my head.

"I know I pushed you toward him. I know that the feelings between you are partly my fault." His Adam's apple jerked up and down, and he suddenly looked at me. The desolation in his eyes melted my insides.

"Jacob—"

"I will bear it if I have to," he growled, his voice ragged, "but I will *not* give you up." His hand at my back pressed harder. "I cannot."

I smiled at him. I couldn't help it. I adored him, but it was rather nice to see him quietly rage with jealousy. "I don't care for Theo. Perhaps as a friend, but nothing more. You're the one I love."

He blinked rapidly and one corner of his mouth tilted upward. He sucked in a breath as deep as the one he'd first gasped after re-awakening in the storage room. "I want to take you somewhere quiet right now and kiss you. Do you think anyone would notice if we disappeared?"

"I think a few might." I giggled and he grinned. Indeed, there was no escaping for us. Still everyone's gaze was on us, some openly, others not quite so obvious.

A little while later, Jacob and I found ourselves separated once again. He was so tall, however, that I could make out his head over the top of everyone else's. Every once in a while he looked for me and when he spotted me, would smile, then turn back to speak to whomever had his attention.

I made my way into the refreshment room where Celia and Louis spoke quietly to one another in the corner, perhaps discussing their upcoming move to Melbourne. They'd been inseparable all week, and now that I knew they were my parents, I couldn't bear to watch them together. I suppose it was sweet, but they were my parents! Did they have to fawn over one another in public?

I was inspecting the array of bonbons, ices and, cakes on the table when a loud whisper caught my attention, which I suspect was the intention.

"I've heard her called pretty," said a young lady seated near the door. She was speaking to two gentlemen hovering near her like bees around a honey pot. She was quite the beauty with curling golden hair, rosy cheeks, and the sort of face men wrote poetry about. From the proud lift of her chin and the fluttering of her lashes, I suspected she knew it too. "Do either of *you* find her pretty?"

"She's tolerably pretty, I suppose," one of the gentleman said with a lazy drawl. "If you like that sort of thing."

"You mean exotic?" the girl replied in her throaty whisper.

"Exotic?" the other gentleman said. "You call that...*thing* exotic?" The biting sneer cut clear through the room. He wasn't even trying to keep his voice low. "She looks like a savage, fresh off the ship. And she's quite mad, I believe. Thinks she can see ghosts, don't you know." He laughed as if he were sharing a joke with his friends.

But it was no joke. He spoke loudly enough for me to hear every word. I looked down at the table, but it blurred and my fingers fumbled with the cake. But I would not cry. Not here. Not now. I refused to give him the satisfaction.

"Of course, she was caught out as a fraud recently," he went on. "Don't know why Lord Preston allows her into his house. He ought to have his chums at Scotland Yard investigate her. Best place for her is in—"

His tirade ended with a gurgle. I turned and saw Jacob clutching the man's necktie. He'd lifted him a clear inch off the floor.

"You do NOT speak about her like that," Jacob growled. A pulse throbbed in his tightly clamped jaw. "Not in my presence, nor out of it. She's a better person than you will ever be, Littleton, and she's the most beautiful woman I've ever seen. If you dare speak of her in such a way again, I will throttle you." He gave the man a shake. "Understand?"

Littleton's face turned a bright shade of purple and his eyes bulged dangerously. He nodded quickly, as best he could, and squeaked, "Yes, yes!"

I placed a hand on Jacob's arm. "Come and have some lemonade with me," I said gently.

He lowered Littleton who tugged at his tie and cleared his throat. Jacob turned fierce eyes on me. He was still seething with anger, but it was slowly dampening as I held his gaze, silently willing him to be calm once more.

I was about to steer him away when his mother sailed up to us. From the harried look on her face, I suspect she must have witnessed what had happened or been told about it. She gave Jacob an admonishing frown, which he didn't seem to notice, and smiled sweetly at me.

"I think this might be a good time to tell everyone about your engagement, Jacob," she said in a sing-song voice that reminded me of Celia and how she would pretend everything was all right when it was not.

"Engagement?" the young lady seated by the door said. Her hand fluttered at her chest and for a moment I thought she might burst into tears, so forlorn did she look.

"Yes," Jacob said in a voice that didn't hide the fact he was still angry. He took a deep breath and the tension seemed to leave his body. He clasped me suddenly round the waist and hooked me into his side. It felt so right to be there. Perfect.

His mother gasped. "Jacob," she hissed, "everyone can see you."

"I know," he said, breaking into a grin. "That's the whole point. I want to give them something scandalous to talk about." He tipped me back and kissed me on the mouth. It was a shocking thing to do in public. Gentlemen of Jacob's ilk were not supposed to show affection toward anyone except in private, but he didn't seem to notice the gasps and his mother's protests.

I certainly didn't care. I was consumed by that kiss. Totally, absolutely devoured by the love of my life. The kiss was thorough and possessive, staking his claim, an attempt to show everyone that I was his. I reached up and wrapped my arms around his neck, holding him to me. He felt so solid and tasted delicious, and I let him kiss me until I was boneless.

I expected his father to stride up and attempt to wrench us apart, but instead, something quite different happened.

Somebody clapped. Then another joined it, and another. Before long, the applause became deafening.

Jacob grinned against my mouth. "I love you, Miss Emily Chambers. And now the world knows it."

WANT MORE EMILY AND JACOB?
LOOK OUT FOR

The Wrong Girl

Book #1 in the 1st FREAK HOUSE TRILOGY.

Eight years after the end of EVERMORE, Emily, Jacob and other characters from the Emily Chambers Spirit Medium Trilogy appear in the Freak House series. THE WRONG GIRL, the 1st book in the First Freak House Trilogy, is now available for immediate download. Read on for an excerpt of THE WRONG GIRL at the end of this ebook.

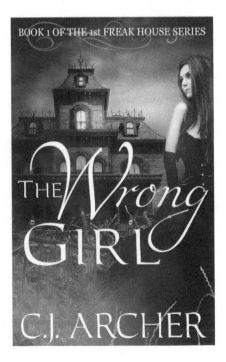

Books by C.J. Archer:

The Wrong Girl (Freak House #1)

Playing With Fire (Freak House #2)

The Charmer

The Medium (Emily Chambers Spirit Medium #1)

Possession (Emily Chambers Spirit Medium #2)

Evermore (Emily Chambers Spirit Medium #3)

Her Secret Desire (Lord Hawkesbury's Players #1)

Scandal's Mistress (Lord Hawkesbury's Players #2)

To Tempt The Devil (Lord Hawkesbury's Players #3)

Honor Bound (The Witchblade Chronicles #1)

Kiss Of Ash (The Witchblade Chronicles #2)

Courting His Countess

Redemption

Surrender

The Mercenary's Price

To be notified when C.J. has a new release, sign up to her newsletter. Send an email to cjarcher.writes@gmail.com

ABOUT THE AUTHOR

C.J. Archer has loved history and books for as long as she can remember and feels fortunate that she found a way to combine the two by making up stories. She has at various times worked as a librarian, IT support person and technical writer but in her heart has always been a fiction writer. C.J. spent her early childhood in the dramatic beauty of outback Queensland, Australia, but now lives in suburban Melbourne with her husband and two children.

She has written numerous historical romances for adults. Visit her website www.cjarcher.com for a complete list.

She loves to hear from readers. You can contact her in one of these ways:
Email: cjarcher.writes@gmail.com
Twitter: www.twitter.com/cj_archer
Facebook: www.facebook.com/cjarcher.writes

CPSIA information can be obtained
at www.ICGtesting.com
Printed in the USA
LVHW030951101121
702905LV00001B/202

9 780987 337252